KU-651-394

SEVEN SLASH RANGE

Bennett Foster

CHIVERS

British Library Cataloguing in Publication Data available

This Large Print edition published by BBC Audiobooks Ltd, Bath, 2010.
Published by arrangement with Golden West Literary Agency.

U.K. Hardcover ISBN 978 1 408 45766 5
U.K. Softcover ISBN 978 1 408 45767 2

Copyright © 1936 by Bennett Foster
Copyright © renewed 1964 by Bennett Foster

All rights reserved.

Printed and bound in Great Britain by
CPI Antony Rowe, Chippenham and Eastbourne

CONTENTS

CAST OF CHARACTERS

CODY VENTURE . . . U. S. Marshal and ex-cowhand, in the dirtiest deal of his gun-slinging life.

TIM AULIFFE . . . owner of the Seven Slash—and damned if he'd tear it down!

TIMMY AULIFFE . . . his fiery young daughter.

BRADFORD . . . Auliffe's neighbor, owner of the Circle B, and waiting like a vulture for the fences to fall.

CLAY STEVENS . . . Bradford's foreman, with interest in other people's cattle and women.

BURT RANDALL . . . Circle B hand, in cahoots with Stevens.

WIG PARSONS . . . another Circle B rider, half naked without his guns.

SAM PENDERGAST . . . he peace-officered the whole Arizona Territory.

SCOTT McGUIRE . . . deputy sheriff of Bowie with a unique method of rounding up posses.

VERNE RICHARDS . . . sheriff of Cochise county, with scars from his Tombstone days.

JUAN de CESPEDES . . . a fighting man of a fighting family.

FELIPE de CESPEDES . . . Juan's brother, cow-boss of the THS outfit.

WYATT BROWN . . . just a storekeeper, but keen for a fight.

BILL LONGEE . . . Seven Slash cook, crotchety and broken-down and terribly thirsty.

BUD JESSOP . . . saloon-keeper.

TONY ARPARGO and TOM BEAUMONT . . . a couple of Circle B gun-toters.

CHAPTER ONE

The President's Proclamation

Sitting in the deep stock saddle, giving easily to the easy gait of the horse, Cody Venture fitted perfectly into the time and the setting. There was little to differentiate him from any other rider of the flats. Five feet ten inches tall, a hundred and sixty pounds in weight, his flat-muscled body was as resistant to heat and wind and fatigue as the body of one of the tawny mountain lions that haunted the Chiricahuas. His face, with its high cheek bones, aquiline nose, and firm, thin lips beneath the wide-set grey eyes, was as impassive as that of an Apache. Blue Levi Strauss overalls and a faded blue shirt partially concealed by an unbuttoned vest covered his body; flat-crowned, wide-brimmed Stetson, and rather small, neat boots completed the ensemble. There were spurs on the boots and on the vest that swung open with a sudden puff of air there was a small gold shield. Save for these no metal showed on the man. The spurs were simply custom; Walking John, the big bay gelding, would have been surprised and pained had they been used. The little gold shield told the initiated that its wearer was a Deputy United States Marshal.

Walking John swung to follow the road as it circled the black-jack oaks, and from among the black boles of the trees a heavy cow, her calf beside her, looked out anxiously.

There were other cattle among the black-jacks. Automatically, with eyes that had watched cattle for twenty-six years, Cody noted these. Their condition was good. They were heavy cattle. Shorthorn bulls had fathered the calves that followed at the flanks of the longhorned cows. One of those bulls, a wide-backed roan, paused a moment as if to dispute the trail, and then moved slowly aside.

Cody reached into a vest pocket for tobacco and papers, produced them and began the forming of a cigarette. He was on familiar ground. These oaks had been a playground for him. He lit his cigarette and leaned forward, both hands on the saddle horn, as Walking John stopped at a water hole. As the big bay drank, sucking in the water thirstily, another horse and rider came through the trees. At sight of Cody the newcomer raised a shrill shout, kicked back with spurred heels, and came on at a gallop. Walking John lifted his head, then, assured that an acquaintance was approaching, again lowered his muzzle to the pool. The galloping horse slid to a stop and its rider, fair hair flying, threw herself from the saddle.

'Cody!' she exclaimed, the warmth of welcome in her tone, 'whatever brought you

2

out here?'

A slow smile lit the still, almost harsh, outlines of Venture's face. He slid down from his saddle and, rein in hand, pulled up his horse's head and started around the little pool. 'Ain't that a welcome?' he drawled, his voice deep. 'I come aridin' away out here from Wilcox an' all my best girl can ask me is why I came.'

The girl laughed. Her piquant face lifted to Venture's as he stopped beside her, for she too had flung herself from the saddle. 'If you came to see me you've been a long time doing it,' she challenged. 'You haven't been out here for two months, Cody. Big Tim was talking about it yesterday.'

'I've been busy, Timmy.' Cody's face sobered. 'Is Big Tim at the house?'

The girl frowned. 'He is,' she said. 'Why are you forever and eternally all business, Cody? Aren't you glad to see me? Why do you have to ask about Big Tim just as soon as you leave your saddle?'

Cody shook his head. 'Because I've come to see Big Tim,' he said gently. 'Let's ride up to the house. You can tell me the news on the way.'

The girl was petulant. She turned her small, shapely back on the man, mounted her horse and swung the animal. Cody, too, stepped up on his gelding. Walking John tossed his head. The girl was already in motion.

3

'I don't care whether you're glad to see me or not,' she threw defiantly over her shoulder.

Cody did not reply. Protestations of affection were useless under the circumstances. Timmy Auliffe had always had a mind of her own and a temper as well. She came by both honestly from Big Tim Auliffe, her father. Instead of answering verbally, Cody sent his horse along, caught up with the bright sorrel that Timmy was riding, and with Walking John setting his gait with that of the other horse, Cody leaned over and put his hand on Timmy's where it rested on the saddle horn.

For an instant Cody thought that Timmy Auliffe would shake off his hand. Then she half turned her head and a smile began to form. 'Darn you, Cody,' she said impulsively. 'I like you anyhow!' They both laughed and the tension was broken.

The black-jacks thinned. The dry stream-bed swung away to the left. The two young riders rounded a point at the instant that they reached the edge of the black-jacks, and there before them was Bonita Canyon and the Seven Slash.

The ranchhouse was built of logs, low and spreading, its shake roof dropping wide eaves over the sides. Across the front was a porch, deep and shaded even in the early afternoon sun. The building faced southwest as though to catch all the light possible. Behind the ranchhouse was a bunkhouse, built of rocks.

4

Originally it had been the ranch building and in Apache days, not many years past, had withstood more than one siege. There were corrals and a barn and sheds adjacent to the bunkhouse. A windmill creaked fitfully and water made a flat pattering sound as it poured from the pipe into a rock tank. There were a few cows in one corral and in another five or six horses milled uneasily, staying as far from the west fence as possible. A big man sat on the fence and in the corral a rider, rope in hand, moved easily and warily toward the horses.

'Johnny Bowen is going to start broncs for Tim this year,' announced Timmy as she turned her horse toward the corral. 'There are some good horses in there, Cody. There's one as good as Walking John.'

The big bay gelding pricked up his ears at mention of his name and Cody laughed. 'You'll have to show me,' he retorted.

The man on the corral fence, hearing the approaching horses, turned his head. He was a big man, red-faced and with white hair showing beneath his hat. When he identified the riders he swung his feet across the fence, dropped to the ground and strode forward.

'Cody!' he boomed. 'Talk about the devil an' he's sure to show up. How are you, boy?'

Cody slid down from his horse. Timmy swung from her mount and the two joined the big man, Cody seized Auliffe's extended hand

5

and shook it heartily. 'Out on business, Tim,' he said. 'How are the broncs comin'?'

Auliffe grinned. 'Pretty good,' he said. 'When you goin' to quit this marshal business an' come back an' break horses for me? I could use you, Cody.'

Venture's smile was tight. 'Sometimes I'd like to quit,' he answered. 'I guess I can't, though.'

Auliffe grunted. 'You can if you want,' he said, and then, changing the subject, 'How are things in Wilcox?'

'Fair,' Cody shrugged. 'Not much doing there. Maren has gone an' there's a new girl workin' in the restaurant, and that's about all.'

'Is the girl pretty?' Tim Auliffe winked ponderously at Cody and looked out of the corners of his eyes toward his daughter. 'You know, I been on the lookout for a housekeeper around here for a long time. If I could find the right one I might marry her an' . . .'

'Dad!' Timmy's exclamation interrupted the sentence. 'Whatever are you talking about? You know good and well . . .' She saw that both men were grinning and, realizing that they were teasing her, flushed to the roots of her hair and stamped her foot angrily. 'I think you're both horrid!' she announced wrathfully. 'If you're going to tease I'm going to the house.'

Cody chuckled and Big Tim's laugh boomed. 'We'll be good,' promised the big man, then, turning to Venture: 'So Maren has left the country, huh? Wasn't he the United States Commissioner?'

Cody nodded.

'That leaves you without a boss then,' boomed Auliffe. 'Pretty soft for you: You can stay a month if you want to.'

Cody shook his head. 'I'm on business,' he said briefly. 'I reckon I better tell you, Tim. Theodore Roosevelt has issued an order that all the fences on public domain have to come down.'

Auliffe looked at the young marshal a long second, his face puzzled. 'What's that again?' he asked.

'The President has issued a proclamation that all the fences on government land have to be removed,' explained Cody patiently. 'That's why I rode out, Tim.'

Big Tim Auliffe stood looking at the young officer. From an expression of query his face had changed until it was hard and impassive. His blue eyes blazed angrily. 'You come out to tell me that?' he said levelly.

Cody nodded. Throughout the long ride from Wilcox he had dreaded this instant. Now that it had come he faced Auliffe steadily. 'I had to, Tim,' he said. 'It's part of my job.'

Auliffe stood silent. He stared at Cody Venture as though the young officer were a stranger. When he spoke his voice was low and bitter. 'That means every fence I've got,' he said slowly. 'It means that every damn' Chihuahua cow in the valley can come crowdin' in on my grass. Why, hell! I've been tryin' to build up my cattle. The Chihuahuas will starve 'em out. You know that!'

Cody said nothing. He could hardly bear to look at Big Tim's accusing eyes. Auliffe spoke again.

'Rough Rider Teddy,' he said slowly. 'A friend to the stockman! Hell!'

Still Cody was silent. Auliffe half turned and took two short steps. He wheeled, stepped back, and faced Cody again. 'An' you brought the word out!' he exclaimed. 'You! The kid I raised!'

A slow flush mantled Cody's cheeks. He would have given a good deal to be elsewhere but he stood his ground. 'It was my job, Tim,' he said slowly.

Auliffe's voice raised. 'Damned if I'll do it! Tear down my fences? Not while I'm livin'! I built this place! I worked an' I've fought for it! By God, I can still fight!'

'It's a government order, Tim,' Cody said doggedly. 'I reckon I got to see it enforced.'

Auliffe's face was blood-red. His eyes blazed and taking a step forward he half raised his clenched fist. 'You! . . .' he began, but got no further.

Timmy seized his arm. Gripping her father she whirled to face Cody Venture. There was biting scorn and anger in her voice as she

8

spoke. 'You'd better go,' she said coldly. 'You've done enough damage. Come, Tim! Come on to the house!'

Auliffe hesitated. For a moment he stood poised, a powerful figure of a man. Then he seemed to slump. The strength flowed from him and he was suddenly old. Without another word he turned and with Timmy's hand still on his arm started toward the ranchhouse. Within a few steps he stumbled and the girl helped him catch himself. Cody Venture, his face worn, watched the two. When they entered the house he turned and walked slowly to his horse.

'Enough damage,' he said wearily as he picked up the trailing bridle reins. 'I guess . . .' He swung up on Walking John and wheeling the horse rode slowly toward the gate.

At the open gate he stopped. The man who had been working horses in the corral was at the fence, staring out through the poles. At the house there was no sign of life. Both Timmy and Big Tim had gone in. Cody hesitated. There was a great deal that he wanted to tell Big Tim. There was a time limit on the fence order. Tim should know of that. There were penalties for not obeying. All these things Tim should be told, but—and Cody let a long breath go—there was no use talking to Tim in his present state of mind. No use talking to Tim or Timmy. Cody sighed again. Timmy! Cody Venture was just beginning to realize

9

that Timmy Auliffe, the girl that Big Tim had wanted to be a boy, was not just a kid that he used to play with. She was a woman.

Walking John tossed his head impatiently and Cody rode on toward where the sun was creeping down to the Dragoon Mountains.

Cody had yet another stop to make that day. Out in the valley, fifteen miles from the Seven Slash was another cow outfit. A man named Bradford had recently moved into the territory and bought the Circle B. Cody had not met the man, knew nothing about him, but he did know that he had to stop at the Circle B and inform its owner of President Roosevelt's order. He sent Walking John along toward the black-jacks.

It took Cody a little less than three hours to reach the Valley ranch. Riding out across the valley, he looked at the cattle. He had come down past Helen's Dome, between the Dos Cabezas, and the Chiricahuas. Now he was riding due west. He shook his head at what he saw. The range was dry and yet it was crowded with longhorned Chihuahua cattle. They had been re-branded. For the most part their original brand had been THS, the Terrazas' brand, but they had been vented to the Circle B and to a D Cross. Cody did not know the D Cross. It was new to him.

The brands, while they were interesting, were not of prime importance. What was important was the fact that Big Tim had

10

spoken truthfully. The Seven Slash cattle, heavy and carrying a big strain of shorthorn blood, could not compete with these lean wild cattle from below the line. The Chihuahua cattle, once the fence was down, would move in and take the good grass of Bonita Canyon and the other grass-filled canyons along the west side of the Chiricahuas. The notice that Cody had served on Tim Auliffe was the notice of the death of the Seven Slash.

It was late when Cody reached the Circle B. There were, perhaps, two more hours of light. Cody rode into the yard of the ranch, dismounted, and leaving his reins trailing went toward the house. There was a man on the porch and he arose as Cody approached.

Venture stopped, pushed back his hat and addressed the small, grey-haired man who stood, holding his glasses in his right hand and a paper in the other.

'Mr. Bradford?' inquired Cody.

The man on the porch nodded.

'My name's Venture.' Cody proceeded to business at once. 'I'm Deputy United States Marshal for this district. I came out to see about your fences.'

Bradford inclined his head. 'Won't you come up on the porch, Mr. Venture?' he invited, and when Cody had mounted the steps Bradford gestured toward a chair.

'Now what is this about fences?' he inquired.

11

Cody seated himself and removed his hat. Leaning forward he stated the purpose of his visit.

'President Roosevelt has issued a proclamation that all fences must come down off government land,' he said. 'Have you any fences, Mr. Bradford?'

Bradford, seated, replaced his glasses on his nose and put the ends of his thin fingers together. 'No,' he said, considering his finger tips, 'I haven't. We have a horse pasture fenced and one other small pasture. I happen to own all the land under fence.'

'That's good.' Cody nodded his approbation. 'Then you won't have any trouble.'

'No.' Bradford looked sharply at his visitor. 'I have a neighbor who has a good deal of land under fence, however: government land.'

'Tim Auliffe?' Cody asked. 'I was over there.'

'I'm glad to hear it.' Bradford pursed his lips a little. 'I was in Wilcox not long ago and I stopped at the land office. I looked up Mr. Auliffe's holdings.'

'So?' Cody was interested.

'Yes. Practically his entire ranch is public domain. I'm very glad for this order, Mr. Venture. It's time that men like Auliffe were restrained from seizing everything they can take.'

Cody was a little surprised at the comment.

12

He made no reply, realizing that Bradford would shortly satisfy his curiosity.

Bradford did so. 'My foreman tells me,' he continued, 'that all the best grass, in fact, about all the grass there is close to here, is inside Auliffe's fence.'

'That's right,' said Cody. 'He's got the best range along the mountains.'

'Then it's time he was forced to remove his fences.' Bradford moved his hands in a gesture of finality.

Cody squinted thoughtfully out across the shadow-strewn flats. 'I don't know,' he said finally. 'Tim Auliffe has been here a good while. He's helped settle up the country; in fact, he and some others like him, made it. It comes kind of hard. Auliffe has always looked at that land like it was his own. There aren't many fences in the country, Mr. Bradford. There's room enough for all.'

'Not for land hogs like Auliffe,' stated Bradford flatly. 'With a few more like him there wouldn't be room for anyone.'

'It all depends on how you look at it,' Cody began. 'Now you're from the East, I take it. You . . .'

'From Boston,' interrupted Bradford. 'No, Mr. Venture. I know how you Westerners look at this, but I can't see your viewpoint. I have practiced law for a good many years. I know the law of property rights and title and I do not see where Auliffe has a leg to stand on. My foreman . . .'

In turn Cody interrupted. 'Just who is your foreman?' he asked. 'Seems to me you take his word for quite a lot.'

'I have to take his word for a good deal. I'm not a practical cowman. My foreman is Clay Stevens.'

Cody got slowly to his feet. 'Clay Stevens,' he said, drawing the words. 'So he's your foreman? Well, Mr. Bradford, I reckon I done my errand. I'll be ridin'.'

'It is late.' Bradford, too, rose to his feet. 'You had better stay, Mr. Venture. You . . .'

'No.' Cody shook his head with finality. 'No, I'll go on. Good day, sir.'

He bowed slightly to Bradford, turned his broad back and walked down the steps. As he reached the bottom a man came around the corner of the house, stopped short, and seeing Cody, jerked his hand back until it rested on the gun at his hip.

'Venture!' He spat out the word.

Cody did not pause in his even stride. With his left hand he held the edge of his vest. His right swung easily. Only his eyes were fixed on the man at the corner of the house.

'Stevens.' Bradford's voice was imperative. 'Come here!'

Cody reached Walking John, stopped and half turned. Stevens dropped his hand from his gun butt, paused, watching Cody narrowly, and then, reluctantly, turned and went to the steps.

14

Cody watched him go, then caught the bridle reins and, putting them around Walking John's neck, found a stirrup and swung up.

CHAPTER TWO

The Circle B

Walking John's black tail had barely disappeared through the cottonwoods that lined the yard, before Bradford spoke sternly to his foreman.

'What do you mean, Stevens?' he snapped. 'You acted as though you were a madman. I've told you that I do not want trouble on the Circle B. I've told you that I disapproved of the men wearing guns, and yet you stood there at the house corner with your hand on your pistol as though you expected to use it at any moment. Now I want to know why!'

Stevens, tall, lean and powerful, overtopping Bradford by six inches, shifted nervously from one booted foot to the other. His eyes, close set beneath thin brows, moved furtively from side to side.

'You wouldn't understand, Mr. Bradford,' he began. 'There's been trouble between me an' Cody Venture. I wasn't lookin' to start anythin' but I wasn't goin' to have him get the best of me.'

15

Bradford shook his head. 'I'll tell you for the last time that I don't want trouble on the Circle B,' he said, impressing each word with a forefinger that tapped his foreman's chest. 'I won't have it! That's all! Furthermore, I want this place to stop looking like an arsenal! I'm tired of this constant display of weapons. You can tell the men that the next one I find wearing a gun is discharged!'

Stevens appeared to consider the order. 'You mean you don't want 'em to carry saddle guns neither?' he asked slowly. 'There's coyotes an' lion an' the Lord knows what else, an' every one of 'em eats beef. The boys won't take kindly to not carryin' a rifle on their saddles.'

'I don't mean that they shan't carry rifles.' Bradford shook his head. 'They can carry rifles when they are riding, but I do not want any more of this pistol business.'

Stevens grunted. 'I'll tell 'em,' he said.

Bradford, having given his orders, stood meditating for a moment. 'What was it you wanted to see me about?' he questioned abruptly.

'About them two east wells,' answered Stevens readily. 'Burt Randall just come in from there an' he says that what little grass there was is gone, both at the tanks an' at Pinto wells. Do you want that we should throw them cattle there back to the west, or . . .'

'I want the cattle left just where they are.'

16

Bradford was curt. 'You told me that the range would carry the animals we put on it; otherwise I shouldn't have bought them.'

Stevens kicked the scuffed toe of his right boot against his left heel. 'It would,' he said, 'if we had all the range we got comin' to us. Them wells are right against Auliffe's fence, an' . . .'

'That fence is coming down,' interjected Bradford. 'The President has issued his order. I knew it was coming. My friends in the East keep me informed. In fact, I probably know more about it than the man who just brought me the word. How many men can you spare from range work, Stevens?'

Clay Stevens was caught unprepared by the question. He shifted his weight again and then answered carefully. 'We ain't carryin' any too many,' he said. 'I might spare a couple of boys for a day or two.'

Bradford frowned. 'Then we'll have to hire more men,' he announced decisively. 'When I heard that this fence order was coming I wrote for the details. Where there are fences on public lands the owner can remove them within a given period. If he does not, the fences are taken down by contract and the owner pays the bill. I have bid for the contract in this district.'

'Then you don't figure that Auliffe will pull his own fences?' Stevens kept his voice level with an effort.

'I do not. I want a crew of men and a wagon that I can use when I get that contract.'

Stevens nodded. 'Want me to hire 'em?' he asked.

'Not right away. I'll tell you when I want the men. In the meantime, don't move those cattle. When Auliffe's fences are removed there will be plenty of grass east of us.'

'Yes, sir. Was there anythin' else, Mr. Bradford?'

Bradford thought a moment and then shook his head. 'That's all,' he answered. 'I'll tell you when I want you to get a crew for the work on the fences.'

Stevens ducked his head and turned abruptly on his high heels. He wanted to get back to the bunkhouse. His boot heels clumped as he went down the three steps from the porch.

Bradford watched his foreman disappear around the corner of the building and then settled himself back in his chair and picked up the paper he had been reading. Holding the paper lax in his hands he looked out at the vista before him. The sun had slipped down behind the hills. The valley was blue with haze. The wind had gone and clouds were hovering over the tops of the Dragoons. Bradford smiled. This was living! This was the thing he had always wanted to do. For fifty years he had lived close in the confines of a town. It was good to throw off the fetters of a cramped civilization. His mind flashed back in retrospect. A ranch owner, an Arizona ranchman! Bradford's smile broadened.

From the cookshack came the clangor of a beaten dishpan, and a hoarse voice bawled unintelligibly. Bradford got up, put down his paper and went into the house to see what his own Chinese cook had to offer in the way of a meal.

* * *

Stevens, when he left Bradford, hurried to the bunkhouse. Most of the Circle B crew were in. There were four men at line camps to the west but the other men, six in all, were clustered around the wash bench or were squatting along the wall of the adobe bunkhouse. All were waiting for the supper summons. Stevens singled out a man with his eyes, nodded, and went into the bunkhouse.

The man he had summoned got up slowly, threw away a half-smoked cigarette, and followed the foreman.

Stevens was at the far end of the single room of the bunkhouse. He had thrown his hat on a bunk and was standing beside a window.

'Looks pretty good, Burt,' he said thinly.

Burt Randall tossed his own hat beside Stevens' and joined the foreman at the window. 'What'd the old man have to say?' he asked.

'Said not to move the stuff from the east.' Stevens seated himself on a bunk and Randall sat down beside him. Randall was not as old as Stevens nor as tall. He was thickset with stocky, powerful shoulders. In the semi-gloom of the bunkhouse those shoulders looked immense.

'Not to move 'em, huh?'

'No. Bradford had it figgered right. The order's come down from Washington to tear down the fences.'

'Yeah. How'd you hear?'

'Bradford told me. Cody Venture, damn him, brought out the word today. The old man is figgerin' that he can get a contract to pull fences.'

'Huh?' Randall did not understand.

'They're goin' to let contracts to take down fences that the owners don't pull. Bradford thinks Auliffe won't pull his.'

'An' then what?'

'Then we take a crew an' pull 'em for him!' Stevens' smile was malignant.

'Auliffe will fight!' Randall was a little doubtful.

'Let him. He'll be fightin' the government. That damn' Venture will have to back us up.'

'Did you see Venture?'

'Yeah. He backed off like a scared pup. I tell yuh, Burt, we got things comin' just like we want 'em. There's only one thing wrong. I tried to talk the old man into gettin' some more

20

Chihuahuas an' he won't do it.'

'Well?'

'Well, we'll get 'em. I'm goin' to have enough hungry cows along that fence so when it comes down every damn' Seven Slash beef will starve to death.'

Randall laughed sharply. 'You sure hate Auliffe's guts,' he stated.

'I got reason to.'

For a moment the two were silent, then Stevens broke the quiet. 'Bradford is a damn' fool, Burt; he thinks he's a big ranchman.'

Burt Randall revolved the statement in his mind. 'I still don't figger it all,' he said finally. 'I can't . . .'

'That's why you're workin' for me in place of me for you. Look: If Auliffe fights Bradford, what will happen?'

'I can tell you easy. Bradford will get killed unless we look out for him.'

'Suppose Bradford does get killed? Then what?'

'Then yo're runnin' his ranch.'

'An' Auliffe goes to jail.'

'Mebbe.'

'An' mebbe not.'

Randall nodded his head slowly. 'You got a long head on yuh, Clay.'

'I have to have one. Now tomorrow I'm goin' in to Bowie. There's three, four boys there I want to see.'

Again Randall nodded. 'An' I keep things

goin',' he said. 'OK, Clay.'

There was a strident clangor of noise from the cookshack. Both men rose.

'You keep things goin'!' Clay Stevens reiterated his segundo's words. 'That's right. I reckon we better go see what that grub wrecker has got for supper an' I got a nice surprise for the boys. The boss give orders that they got to shed their guns.' He laughed again, mirthlessly, and led the way to the bunkhouse door.

The other members of the crew were already around the table in the cookshack when Stevens and Randall came in. The two found places, filled their tin plates and fell to eating. Save for smacking lips and the scrape of utensils on plates or against cups, there was no noise. The crew of the Circle B were not a loquacious lot. With the first edge of hunger gone there began to be a little talk.

Stevens, looking up from his place at the end of the table, grinned sardonically at his crew and broke the news of Bradford's recent order. 'The boss says you all got to quit totin' guns,' he announced. 'Says that the damn' place looks like an arsenal an' he don't like it.'

Flat silence greeted the words. Every eye around the table was fixed on Stevens. Six impassive faces waited for the next words.

Stevens' grin broadened. 'Yeah,' he continued. 'Just a lot of sheep-herders, that's us. We can pack saddle guns, but that's all. I told Bradford we had to protect ourselves against coyotes an' such.'

Still there was no comment from the men of the crew. They were waiting for Stevens or Randall to lead the way. These were selected men. Stevens had hired them. They were hand-picked. While they drew Bradford's wages and rode Circle B horses they were loyal only to Stevens. They knew him, and Bradford was a stranger, a 'damned dude.'

'You look mighty solemn, boys,' observed Randall.

Wig Parsons, so called because of his mop of hair, turned and looked at the segundo. 'What's the rest of it?' he asked, his voice dry. 'Go ahead an' spring the cracker. I'd look pretty without a gun an' I'd feel the same way. Hell! I'd be half naked.'

Stevens laughed. 'There's ways an' ways,' he announced. 'Some of you boys got shoulder holsters. Some of you have packed a gun in your pants before this. *I'm* not tellin' you what to wear an' what not to wear.'

Eyes lowered again to look at plates and the business of eating was resumed. Bradford's order had been delivered.

When the meal was finished the men rose, stepped back over the benches, and depositing their dishes in a pan, strolled outside. There they squatted down, backs against the cookshack wall, rolled cigarettes and lit them. Low, monotonous voices spoke briefly as

23

Bradford's order was discussed. Stevens, finishing among the last, joined Burt Randall and the two strolled a little apart from their fellows.

Randall was uneasy. 'I don't like it, Clay,' he said. 'Bradford's gettin' along too fast. When he come he was green as a gourd but he's pickin' up, day by day.'

Stevens shrugged. 'Pickin' up what?' he demanded.

'The layout of the whole thing. We got D Cross cattle scattered from hell to breakfast with his stuff. You know that.'

'An' just how will Bradford make a count?' Clay's voice was contemptuous. 'He couldn't count ten steers an' come out twice alike.'

'How many of them D Cross cattle ought to be wearin' the Circle B?' Randall faced his companion as he asked the question. There was a different timbre in his voice as he asked the question, some challenging note.

Stevens caught it. His drawl was slow as he replied. 'Why do you want to know, Burt?'

'Because I want to. Look here, Clay! You can't play this alone. You hired me an' I'm drawin' wages. I been thinkin'. I want more than that. When the blow-off comes I don't aim to be just a thirty-dollar-a-month cowhand.'

Again Stevens spoke casually. 'Don't worry, Burt. You won't be.'

'Then I'll cut a pardner's share?'

24

'You'll cut a share, all right.'

Randall was insistent. 'I got to know how much,' he said. 'I been goin' blind too long. I want to know where I stand.'

For an instant, blind, unreasoning rage filled Clay Stevens' mind. Burt Randall had been getting out of hand for a long time. Stevens had known that. In that second when he made his declaration, Randall bordered upon instant death. Then Stevens calmed. He knew that he could not kill Randall, not at the Circle B. It would spell his own finish there. With an effort he controlled himself.

'You stand Ace High, Burt,' he said levelly. 'My word on it.'

Randall appeared satisfied. 'That's all I want, Clay,' he announced. 'Yore word's good with me.'

'You got my word that you'll cut a share,' Stevens repeated. 'I'm goin' up to the house now an' talk to Bradford some. I want his orders to go to Bowie tomorrow.'

'Bowie?'

'Yeah. I've decided that you an' me will leave early.'

Randall's eyebrows went up in interrogation. 'You an' me?' he asked.

'We likely won't be back for three, four days,' said Stevens. 'Wig can run things, Burt.'

'I guess he can, at that.' Randall nodded and half turned. 'Just one thing, though, Clay: Don't you cross me up. Don't you do that!'

'You got my word,' said Stevens, and started toward the house.

CHAPTER THREE

The Way to Get a Posse

When he left the Circle B Cody rode due north-west. His mind was filled with conjecture and surmise. So filled, that his visit to the Seven Slash was almost relegated to the background. Cody Venture knew Clay Stevens, knew him well. Stevens had not been in the Sulphur Springs Valley for three years. Three years ago Cody, Tim Auliffe, and certain other ranchmen of the Valley and the Chiricahuas had convinced Stevens that for the good of his health he had best leave. There had been various things that had brought this about. Cattle and horses had been stolen and while their theft could not be traced directly to Stevens, it was noticeable that the thievery had ceased with his departure. The thing that had put Venture against Stevens, however, was not the rustling but rather the fact that Stevens had insulted Timmy Auliffe.

There had been a dance at Lance Blount's place near Portal. Timmy had been there, as had Big Tim, Cody, and many others. Blount, with true hospitality, had furnished a keg of whisky with a tin cup to bail it out, and Stevens had visited the keg too often. It was after one of these visits, when Stevens had returned to the dance, that Cody found Timmy Auliffe in tears. Interrogation had brought out nothing but Cody had seen Stevens with the girl shortly before. Reaching a conclusion he had hunted up Stevens, invited him outside and administered a very thorough thrashing. It was shortly after this that public opinion, coupled by a visit from several influential cattlemen who meant what they said, had sent Stevens down the trail.

Riding northwest, Cody recalled all these happenings. The scowl on his face deepened. If Bradford was taking advice from his foreman, Clay Stevens, then every cowman in the valley should be on the alert. Auliffe in particular. Cody swore softly to himself at the thought. Stevens' presence on the Circle B accounted for the number of Chihuahua cattle along Auliffe's fence. Cody could have bet on that. The whole thing was bad and this order from Washington made it worse. The worst part of the whole situation was that Cody himself would be an instrument in Stevens' hand. In his official capacity he was in duty bound to see that the proclamation was obeyed. That, as Cody said to himself, was 'the hell of it.'

When night overtook him he made camp close by a windmill, boiled coffee in a can, taking a supply from a saddle pocket, and with the hot liquid and a cigarette for his supper, and with slicker and saddle blanket for a bed, settled down for the night. He lay on his back, staring up at the stars that seemed to rest just beyond his arm's reach, and revolving the problems of the day over and over. Gradually peace settled on him and he slept.

Morning found Cody on the road again and well before noon he was in Wilcox. He ate a meal there and got his mail. There were official papers in the mail and one letter from the marshal in Tucson. Pendergast, the marshal, wrote that Cody was to come to Tucson immediately. Among the other papers was a summons to be served in Cochise and so, when the noon train of the Southern Pacific whistled for the Wilcox station, Cody Venture was on the platform, waiting.

The trip to Tucson was slow, as usual, and it was night before Cody arrived. He had served the summons in Cochise, having plenty of time while the train stopped. Now in Tucson, he went directly to a hotel, secured a room where he made his toilet, then after eating his supper, went to the marshal's office. The marshal was waiting for him.

Sam Pendergast, United States Marshal for the territory of Arizona, was an old-timer. Lank, tall and white-haired, he rose from his chair when Cody entered the office, and walked around his desk to shake hands. There were two or three men in the office and these greeted the young deputy from Wilcox. Cody found a seat and waited while Pendergast concluded his business, and when the last caller had departed the old marshal turned to his deputy.

'Well,' he said slowly, tipping back in his chair, 'how's it goin', Cody?'

Cody revolved his hat in his hands, looked the marshal straight in the eyes and answered. 'Not so good,' he said. 'I'm goin' to quit this job, Sam, as soon as I get done with the chore I'm on.'

Pendergast nodded. 'I figgered that way,' he said, bringing out a plug of tobacco. 'I run you into a tough spot, Cody.'

Cody was silent while Pendergast chewed off a generous corner of the plug and the marshal continued. 'If you want, I'll move you from Wilcox. I know how it stands between you an' Tim Auliffe an' I know how you feel about him. Mebbe the pressure wouldn't be so great if you moved down to Nogales, say, for a while.'

Cody shook his head. 'I already been out to see Tim,' he announced. 'Most of Tim's fences are on public land.'

'I know that.' The marshal chewed slowly for a moment. 'I've known Tim a long time, Cody.'

Cody made no comment and the old man went on. 'What about movin' you?' he asked.

Again Cody shook his head. 'It wouldn't do any good,' he said bluntly. 'No. I'll stay on an' see this through, an' then I'll quit.'

'But you ain't goin' to quit now?' Pendergast squinted at his visitor.

'No.'

A slow smile spread over the marshal's face. 'I didn't think you would,' he said. 'It ain't in any of Frank Venture's breed to quit. How are things up there?'

Cody considered for a moment. His business with Clay Stevens was purely personal and he could not tell Pendergast of the cattle that crowded against Auliffe's fence. That was not the marshal's concern and as an officer it was no concern of Cody's. Finally he answered.

'Auliffe's goin' to fight this fence order.'

'I thought he would.' Pendergast nodded slowly. 'I don't like it myself. It'll play hell with the range but there ain't nothin' we can do about it. We're here to carry out orders whether we like 'em or not.'

'Yes,' agreed Cody.

'Now I'm goin' to write Tim,' Pendergast continued after a moment's silence. 'I'll tell him just where we stand an' mebbe I can make him understand it. I'd go up there but right now I got other eggs to fry. Who's goin' to be commissioner up there, Cody?'

'I wish I knew.'

'I got no word on that yet. One thing I can

tell you. If the owners don't pull down their own fences, contracts are goin' to be let an' the fences will come down anyhow. Know who's bid on the contract up there?'

Cody shook his head.

'A man named Bradford. Know him?'

'I've met him.'

'You've got to remember this, Cody,' Pendergast drawled his words, 'it'll be up to the deputy marshals to protect these fence contractors. We mebbe will have to put on extra men, but we'll get the job done.'

Pendergast's announcement had set the wheels at work in Cody Venture's head. If Bradford was to have the contract for pulling down fences there was bound to be open war between Auliffe and Stevens, for, no doubt, Stevens would superintend the actual work.

'How long do the owners have to get their wire down?' he asked.

'Three weeks, an' then the contractor takes over.'

The corners of Cody's thin lips drew down in deprecation. 'Then in three weeks I'll have a pretty little fight on my hands,' he announced.

'Probably. You still want to stay up there?'

'I'll stay. I started an' I might as well finish.'

'You want some help?'

'Not yet.'

'Then,' Pendergast rose slowly from his chair, 'I reckon you might as well go get a night's sleep. I'll see you in the mornin'.'

31

He held out his hand. Cody took it and said, 'Good night.' From the marshal's office he went straight to his hotel and to bed.

In the morning Cody went back to the courthouse and spent an hour closeted with Pendergast. The old officer warned Cody to proceed cautiously, gave him good advice and what aid he could, and then other business claimed his attention.

Cody, released, went back downtown and waited for his train. He was uneasy and anxious to get back, and his lean, dark face was moody as he climbed up the steps of the day-coach ready to begin his return journey.

Cody reached Wilcox at four o'clock. He visited the commissioner's office, found that there was nothing there to claim his attention, and went to the livery stable. There he saddled Walking John, and leaving word that he was going to San Simon, pulled out along the dusty road that bordered the Southern Pacific's tracks leading east.

At ten o'clock he reached Bowie and deciding that he had better go on in the morning, put his horse in Summerford's livery barn, ate supper and got a room in the hotel. He was in no mood to talk and went to bed, tired and restless.

Cody Venture did not hear the thump of boot-heels along the hotel's carpetless corridor; did not hear the whirr of spur rowels raking over the boards; but the hearty thump that rattled the thin pine door brought him from his bed all standing. Following the thump the door creaked and swung open; a match flamed and young Venture sat down on his bed, returning beneath his pillow that which he had seized.

'Well,' said Cody.

Scott McGuire's emotionless voice drawled in the darkness that followed the brief flaming of the match. 'Get your clothes on, Cody,' commanded McGuire. 'Get dressed. We're leavin' right out.'

Cody said, 'Huh!' and reached for his trousers.

The flat voice continued. 'The S. P. train with the Douglas payrolls was stopped just below Rodeo, two, three hours ago. They killed the messenger an' the engineer. Word just come from Lordsburg.'

'Light the lamp,' requested Cody who was having difficulty with his shirt sleeves. 'What are you draggin' me in on this for, Scott?'

Scott McGuire, deputy sheriff of Bowie, scratched another match and, crossing the little room, ignited the wick of the lamp on the rickety table. Tall and gaunt, he stepped back from the light and surveyed his questioner with sardonic, light blue eyes. 'I just want you along,' he drawled. 'Git dressed an' don't talk so much.'

Cody got his shirt sleeves sorted out and pulled the blue garment over his head. 'I got

33

troubles of my own, Scott,' he said.

'You got some more now,' returned the deputy.

Cody stamped his feet into the boots, crossed the room and splashed water on his face from an enamelware basin, and subdued his unruly straw-colored hair with three strokes of a comb. Scott McGuire watched the proceedings as he divulged further information.

'Things are already organized below,' he said. 'We'll get right out.'

Cody thrust his left arm through a shoulder holster, pulled the elastic strap across his back and looped it over his right arm. He picked up his vest from the back of a chair, put it on, leaving it unbuttoned, stuck the gun that had been beneath his pillow into the holster, and picked up his hat. 'All right,' he said. 'Who all's goin'?'

'Ain't got 'em yet,' replied McGuire. 'We'll tend to that when we get outside.'

Cody grunted, blew out the light and followed the tall McGuire out the door. As they walked down the corridor, tramped down the stair and emerged upon Bowie's lifeless street, McGuire gave his brother officer the word of what had been done.

'The Rodeo deputy is hittin' for the Animas with a posse,' he said. 'Verne Richards happened to be at Gleason an' he's takin' a bunch from there an' comin' right across.

Toliver is goin' into Dos Cabezas from San Simon an' a posse from Douglas is bottlin' the border.'

Cody reviewed the country briefly in his mind and grunted again. 'That leaves us the Chiricahuas,' he said. 'The whole darn range. Isn't anyone strikin' in from Paradise?'

'Verne will take that,' answered McGuire in the velvet blackness of the street. 'They don't know which way these fellows went. It rained down below Rodeo an' there's no tracks.'

'Well'—Cody stopped and faced toward the voice—'who we goin' to get? Let's get organized.'

McGuire did not reply. There was the sound of a movement in the darkness, three loudly audible clicks and a six-shooter bellowed, once, and then again. Cody found himself in a crouch, his own hand on his gun. Scott McGuire had fired twice.

'What the devil? . . .' began Venture, angrily, coming out of his crouch and dropping his hand.

'That's the easiest way to get a posse in Bowie,' vouchsafed McGuire, the tiny tinkle that accompanied his words telling that he was jacking empties from his single action. 'See! What did I tell you?'

Down the street, a door slammed and then another. From above the Alcatraz Saloon a light showed briefly, a window went up with a bang and the light was blotted out. McGuire moved quickly across toward the lighted building.

'That's Bud Jessop,' he said hastily. 'Better get out of line, Cody. He's got a scatter gun.'

Cody took three quick steps, a voice bellowed from the lighted window, profanely inquiring what was happening, and McGuire lifted his own voice in reply.

'Come on down, Bud, an' bring a lamp. The S. P. has been held up below Rodeo.'

From Cody's immediate left a hammer clicked as it was lowered and a man whose nightshirt made a grey blur, came along the boardwalk under the porch of a store building. 'Did you say the S. P., Scott?' he asked as he stopped.

As McGuire replied more men arrived. Bud Jessop, immense in nightshirt and trousers, came through the door of the Alcatraz carrying a lamp, and the forming group was illuminated. Cody recognized Cal Summerford, the owner of the livery stable and wagon yard, two cowboys from the big Three C outfit that ranged north, Wyatt Brown from Meyers General Store, and the dark face and gleaming teeth of Juan de Cespedes. Scott was giving information and issuing orders.

'I'll want you two Chiricahua boys,' he said after he had briefly reported the robbery, 'an' you, Juan, an' you, Wyatt. Better get saddled right away an' we'll meet at Bud's.'

Bud Jessop grunted profanely and Scott answered the implication. 'You're too damn' big, Bud,' he said. 'You'd bog down a horse. Light up, will yuh? We got to get goin'.'

Jessop turned back into the Alcatraz and Cody followed Summerford toward the livery stable. Others of the group, those who had been summoned, were departing in various directions, the remainder standing close about McGuire and asking questions. Summerford opened the stable doors, lit a lantern that hung just inside, and spoke apologetically to Cody.

'I reckon you can find your horse,' he said. 'Just leave the doors open. I got to go on home. The old lady is standin' by the door with a shotgun an' I reckon I better get back before she spooks at somethin' an' lets go.'

Cody grinned and nodded, and Summerford went on down the street.

When Cody led Walking John from the livery stable he found that Bowie was fully awake. There were lights in the town's few houses and in the Alcatraz there were twenty or twenty-five men. Cody left his horse at the hitch rail and went on in. Two of the possemen had appeared; the two Three C punchers. McGuire had gone to get his horse and Bud Jessop was behind the bar, his chest showing immense and hairy through his unbuttoned nightshirt. Talk concerning the robbery was rife and as Cody stopped inside the room a man returned from the depot bringing fresh news garnered by the night operator.

'They think them fellows have headed over into New Mexico,' said the new arrival importantly. 'The night man just got the word.'

Jessop grinned at Venture. 'I'll bet you hope they have, Cody,' he said familiarly. 'There's enough work in the *Territory* of Arizona, ain't there, without takin' on any of them Grant County bandits?'

Cody nodded his agreement, waved aside the bottle that Jessop shoved across the bar and was reaching for papers and tobacco when the arrival of McGuire with de Cespedes and Wyatt Brown interrupted proceedings. McGuire was ready to start.

'Let's pull out, boys,' he requested. 'It's three o'clock now an' it'll be light by the time we reach the hills. Let's go.'

There were calls of good luck, some roughly humorous remarks, and the five possemen, taking their horses from the Alcatraz hitch rack, mounted and rode down the dark street. At the outskirts of the little town Cody spoke to McGuire who rode beside him.

'That's one way to get a posse, all right,' he said softly.

A match flamed and illuminated McGuire's face as he lit a cigarette. 'An' it's a good way,' he rejoined. 'I been a peace officer a long time an' I've found that if you take the first four or five men who come a-runnin' when there's shots fired, you generally get the pick of the prime beef. Let's shake it up a little, boys.'

For a time thereafter the progress of the five horsemen was marked by the creak of leather and the occasional jingle of a bit chain. A grey flush, faint, barely discernible, marked the beginning of daybreak. The horses followed a steady, rapid walk through mesquite, cactus and creosote bush. As the eastern horizon became pink with morning light, Scott McGuire stirred his horse from the walk into a trot and behind and beside him the others took up the more rapid beat.

'Where first, Scott?' queried Cody, riding beside the deputy sheriff.

'The country around Rough Mountain first,' replied the lanky McGuire. 'Then I reckon we'll work down under Cochise Head an' on to Rustlers' Park.'

Cody nodded and lifted his eyes toward the Chiricahuas, black and forbidding in the morning light. 'Not much chance we'll find 'em,' he said. 'There's lots of country.'

There was a lot of country. It lay spread before the riders of the posse, familiar and yet with always a fresh aspect. South were the towering masses of the Chiricahuas, black, gaunt, their outer walls barren. To the west the Dos Cabezas, two bare-faced rocks, towered above the mountains they named. Beyond the Dos Cabezas the Sulphur Springs Valley spread toward the south and to the east the tops of the Animas caught the morning sun and shone like a forest afire. Somewhere, the riders in Scott McGuire's posse knew, somewhere in that broad reach of savage rocks and equally savage vegetation, were men riding with loot on their saddle horns. Somewhere, too, were other men, bent on the identical errand they themselves pursued. The horses clattered down a rock-strewn knoll, struck the sand of the arroyo at its bottom and, their hoofbeats deadened, began a circuitous traverse of the dead stream-bed.

Cody Venture spoke, half to himself. 'A wild-goose chase,' he said.

'I've shot wild geese,' snapped McGuire. 'This is part of the job.'

They broke from trot to walk and then back to the trot again. How many miles lay ahead they did not know. In this country horses are paramount, all important, and the men that followed Scott McGuire saved their mounts. They climbed out of the arroyo and began a steady ascent of the canyon from which the dry wash came.

At ten o'clock they were in the hills, riding the ridges, scanning the country that lay below and to either side. The area around Rough Mountain yielded nothing and they worked on south. They crossed a little divide between two canyons and began to work down the southern slope. At noon they were below Cochise Head, a mass of rock piled on a mountain top, that, from a distance, traced to perfection the gaunt profile of an Indian lying on his back. There were caves below the Head and the posse worked cautiously. They nooned in the canyon below the Head, horses grazed with loosened cinches and drank from a little stream that barely trickled between deep holes. The men drank from the stream and tightened their belts. They planned to eat that night at Paradise, a mining camp at the southern foot of the mountains.

'Richards ought to be at the south end now,' said Cody to Scott McGuire as they rested their backs against a boulder and puffed on cigarettes.

McGuire nodded. Verne Richards was the sheriff of Cochise County, a hard-bitten, hard-riding individual who had won his spurs in one of Tombstone's lesser wars. 'Just about at Paradise,' assented McGuire. 'I wish we were there. I didn't have no breakfast.'

One of the Three C cowboys laughed at the words and his partner, grinning, asked, 'Who did?'

Juan de Cespedes, Mexican fighting man of a fighting family, sucked slowly on the corn-husk roll he held carefully between his fingers. 'We eat the wind, caballeros,' he said, his voice whimsical. 'Still, I would like one good meal. Who knows? . . .'

McGuire got to his feet. 'Let's get along,' he commanded. 'Likely we'll meet Verne somewhere below an' he might have brung a

41

snack with him.'

Wyatt Brown chuckled. 'I got a picture of Verne doin' that,' he said as he walked toward his horse. 'A coal-oil painting.'

Mounted again they struck on down the canyon. Rustlers' Park, already the scene of one bloody conflict, lay below them. The quiet of the hills, the absence of any life, cattle or game, lay upon them heavily. Somewhere ahead a blue jay chattered raucously and Walking John pricked up his ears.

'Somethin' ahead,' announced McGuire, needlessly. 'Fan out a little, boys.'

Obediently the possemen spread out but the blue jay ceased its clamor, and a red-sided cow above them in the brush sent a rock clattering as she ran. They rode on slowly.

Rustlers' Park appeared around a bend in the canyon. The Park was a natural amphitheater. Hills set about its green bottom, and there was a stream, tiny, but water in an almost waterless country.

'Funny,' said McGuire, 'there's always grass in the Park. Has some seepage to feed it, I reckon.'

Cody was sighting familiar landmarks. 'There's the old corral,' he said. 'Wasn't it there that Old Man Sandham killed Trueblood?'

McGuire nodded and one of the Three C men behind him asked curiously: 'Was you here when they had that mixup, Scott?'

McGuire nodded again. Despite its greenness and freshness, Rustlers' Park held no witchery for him. 'Yeah,' he drawled. 'I was here.'

'How did all that start, Scott?' asked the other Three C cowboy. 'That was before my time in this country. Wasn't there a bunch rustlin' stock from the valley an' holdin' 'em here? I've heard somethin' about it.'

McGuire half turned in his saddle, ready to answer the questioner. Walking John stepped swiftly to the right as a trained horse will to avoid a hole, and from the further side of the Park a shot spanked sharply in the quiet. A slug chugged into the bole of an eight-inch pine tree, close beside Cody.

CHAPTER FOUR

Rustlers' Park

With the flat sound of the shot the posse fanned right and left. Cody, wheeling Walking John back, swung from the saddle, pulling his carbine from the saddle scabbard across the saddle as he dropped down. The big gelding, freed of his rider, took a few steps and then stopped to look back. Cody was on the ground, working rapidly toward the shelter of a boulder-strewn slope. As his horse stopped the young deputy marshal seized a piece of rock and threw it. Walking John, insulted by his master's action, went a few steps farther. Again Cody exposed himself to throw, and again a rock slapped the horse in the ribs. Convinced that he was not wanted, Walking John moved away, the reins trailing. Cody wormed his way on toward the rock pile.

To his right and left other horses were moving back. Not a posseman was visible and down across the green of Rustlers' Park no movement was discernible; yet death lurked in the sunlit quiet. Across the green of the park the brown poles of the tumbledown corral, already the scene of one death by violence, showed stolid and undisturbed. Following that first shot a pregnant silence fell over the scene. There was no sound save steel shoes clinking against rocks as the horses moved back.

Cody, from his vantage point, stared steadily down the slope, the carbine pushed out in front of him. He knew that the other possemen were concealed and watching, just as he was watching. Somewhere down the slope and across the green were other men. It seemed to Cody that there was a little movement in the oak brush that bordered the grass, a movement not caused by wind. He squinted down the barrel of the carbine, finger on the trigger.

To his left and above him a rifle spoke sharply, two whip-like reports shattering the quiet. Close to the corral a tiny flower of smoke bloomed suddenly and was washed away by the breeze. Cody swung the carbine toward that smoke puff and even as he did so saw the movement in the oak brush again. A gun spoke across the park, and gravel and sand spurted at Cody's elbow.

On the slope above him the rifleman found another target and fired rapidly. Two guns answered close by the corral but the man who had been using black powder did not fire. There were at least four men hidden opposite the possemen. A horse moved down the hill slope on Cody's right and the young deputy turned to see Juan de Cespedes rise to his full height and throw a handful of gravel at the animal. It was Juan's horse. Cody wondered if Walking John had moved out of sight; even as the thought flashed through his mind he saw de Cespedes half whirl and go down.

Wyatt Brown's voice came from beyond the spot where Juan had fallen: 'Hit, Juan?'

There was no answer.

Cody's face was lined a little deeper as he resumed his watch. Again there was a movement in the brush. He fired three deliberate shots, the kick of the rifle feeling good against his shoulder.

Wyatt Brown spoke again, closer now, a single word: 'Hell!'

Then Juan de Cespedes was dead! Cody sensed it from the utter finality in Brown's

45

voice. Far to the left the two Three C punchers went suddenly into action. They were shooting pistols and Cody found time to wonder if they did not have rifles with them. Probably not or they would be using them. He was watching the oak brush. There was a brown spot in it that did not just conform. It could not be a tree trunk. Cody fired twice at the brown spot, levering the gun rapidly between shots. At the second report a man crawled out from the oak, moving aimlessly. He crawled a body's length and settled into the green of the park's border to remain motionless.

The rattle of the Three C six-shooters stopped suddenly. Cody wormed his way back from his boulder and started across the little canyon toward where he had last heard Brown. It was time that something was done.

Dust and sand kicked up twice close to him and he hugged the earth. On the far hillside Brown began to fire rapidly, masking Cody's movements. Venture reached another boulder, slid behind it, and Brown stopped shooting.

Cody raised himself cautiously. He was halfway up when he heard Brown shoot again and a rifle to the left echoed the explosion. That rifle would be Scott McGuire's. Cody lifted his right hand and felt of his hat brim. There was a ragged tear in the edge of the Stetson. He had not heard the shot that caused the tear, and he crouched again, trying to peer around his boulder without exposing himself.

He heard Wyatt swear, the words coming in a slow, drawling monotone, and saw Brown get to his feet. Wyatt was above him on the slope. Cody lifted himself and looking back saw a Three C puncher walking across the arid hillside some two hundred yards distant. The Three C man was swinging a Colt. There were no shots from across the Park and Cody got to his feet.

Brown, up the slope, said, 'Juan is dead,' his voice dispassionate.

Scott McGuire rose from concealment and moved toward the Three C puncher. They met and stopped. The Three C man moved his hands rapidly. His words did not carry to Cody. McGuire turned and beckoned. Brown came down the hillside, his rifle across his arm.

'Washout,' he said.

Brown joined Cody and together they walked to where McGuire and the Three C man stood. The other Three C cowboy was approaching from the east. McGuire spoke as Cody and Brown stopped.

'There was four of 'em,' he said. 'There's two dead ones across the park. The other two sloped and got away.'

The Three C puncher spoke plaintively. 'One of you fellers with a rifle should of gone with us,' he said. 'We seen them two movin' but they was too far for a short gun.'

Brown repeated, 'Juan is dead.'

McGuire nodded slowly. 'Somebody will

47

have to take 'em in,' he announced. 'The rest of us will follow 'em. Who was that you hit, Cody?'

'I couldn't see,' replied Cody.

McGuire looked at the men about him. The other Three C puncher approached, his breath short from exertion. 'You Chiricahua boys better 'tend to things here,' McGuire ordered. 'Do what you can. We better be movin'.'

'Where'll we take 'em?' demanded a Three C puncher.

'Portal will be closest, I reckon,' McGuire answered absently. 'Let's get the horses.'

The men separated, stumbling across rock in their high heels. Cody followed back up the little canyon, and around a bend found Walking John standing on a rein. De Cespedes' horse and Brown's mount were with the big bay.

Cody caught Walking John, mounted, and riding close caught the reins of the other two animals and led them down the canyon. Where it opened into the park basin he came upon Wyatt Brown. Brown was carrying a body. Cody stopped and dismounted.

Silently he helped Brown load the limp body of Juan de Cespedes and lash it in place with a saddle rope. Over across the park they say McGuire and the other two possemen ride into view and disappear into the trees again.

'Gone after the horses,' said Brown, needlessly.

'They better hurry,' rejoined Cody.

McGuire and the Three C men reappeared, leading horses. The Three C men stopped beside the edge of the grass and McGuire came on. Brown mounted and took the reins of the lead horse.

'I'll take Juan on across to 'em,' he said apologetically. 'I liked the kid. He was game.'

Cody nodded and Brown rode away across the park. McGuire came on, rode up and stopped. 'Where now, Scott?' questioned Cody.

Scott McGuire frowned absently. 'We'll try to trail 'em,' he said. 'Them fellows was three hundred yards away an' flaggin' it when the boys started shootin'.'

'Too far,' said Cody.

'Too far to even see good who they was. The boys'll take Juan an' them other two on to Portal. They can get a wagon there. Too bad about Juan.'

Silence for a moment. Brown came back across the park at a lope. 'Which way you reckon they went, Scott?' he demanded as he stopped.

'The Lord knows,' replied McGuire. 'There's lots of country.'

Brown said, 'I'm hungry as hell!' plaintively, and Cody reined Walking John around.

'That man you hit was Bill Lomax,' said McGuire, moving his horse abreast of Venture's. 'He's dead. I don't know the other one. Wyatt an' me both hit him when he raised up to shoot at you.'

'We were a little late,' said Brown. 'Look at Cody's hat.'

The three riders moved steadily across the slope. They dropped into a little draw that scored the slope, saw three empty cartridge cases on the sand and knew that they had reached the spot where the Three C man had ejected his empties. Riding on they mounted a low ridge. At the top McGuire halted.

'They crossed this,' he said. 'Here's where the boys saw 'em. They were headed east.' Beyond the hogback was a wide canyon and on the further side mountains loomed again.

Cody shrugged. 'Think we can be lucky twice, Scott?' he asked.

McGuire shook his head. 'We can try,' he said.

They set their horses down the slope. Halfway down they found tracks where horses had pounded across the sandy slope. The tracks led to the canyon. The three followed. Presently rock supplanted the sand and the tracks were lost. McGuire reined in his horse.

'Which way?' questioned Brown.

McGuire shrugged. 'There's two ways out of here. Three ways if they headed back. My guess is that they went on across an' will hit for the Animas.'

'We killed some time back there,' suggested Cody. 'Likely they're quite a ways ahead.'

'We had to tend to those boys,' replied McGuire. 'Which way do you think they went, Cody?'

Cody frowned. Suddenly resolution formed in his mind. 'We can't just go blind,' he announced. 'It's gettin' late. You two go on toward the Animas. You may find somethin'. I'm goin' to head north. There's a line camp just below Maverick Peak an' I'll get somethin' to eat, an' go on.'

McGuire nodded. 'I don't think we'll find 'em either,' he said. 'All right, Cody. Thanks.'

Cody nodded. 'I'll see you, Scott,' he said. 'You, too, Wyatt. So long.'

Wyatt Brown and McGuire echoed the words and moved their horses on down across the rock. Cody, turning Walking John to the left, followed the long slope of the hill toward the canyon bottom. Well down the side he struck a trail and turned the horse into it. Looking back he saw that McGuire and Brown had disappeared.

For an instant Cody was tempted to ride back. It was foolish for the three to split as they had. Then he shook his head. Little chance of finding the two renegades in these hills. A needle in a haystack would be easy to locate in comparison. He might as well ride on to the line camp. Walking John strode steadily along the trail, eating up the distance with the long road gait that had earned him his name.

Cody struck the upper range at the mouth

of Pinery Canyon and followed the trail between the gradually contracting walls. This was all old, familiar ground to him. To his right Maverick Peak reached skyward, a rock-strewn landmark. The sun was dropping swiftly toward the canyon rim. Another two hours would bring dark to the canyon. Five miles of riding from the mouth of the canyon brought him to the trail that turned abruptly to the right and that led to the camp at the foot of the peak. Cody followed it. Walking John was tired. He had covered a good many miles during the day and his gait was slackening. Cody squinted westward. The sun was just at the edge of the rim.

The line camp was a tiny, rock-walled house, half buried in the hillside. Cody stopped, dismounted, and walking to the shack, pushed open the door. There was seldom a rider at the Maverick camp. There was none there now. Cody, walking into the dark room, struck a match and searched the shelf that hung from the ceiling. The pack rats could not come down the wires that held the shelf and food placed upon it was comparatively safe. There were dry beans on the shelf, a can of corn and a can of tomatoes. Cody took the corn and the tomatoes and went out. He would repay the borrowed goods at some later visit.

Out by his horse again Cody cast a look skyward and decided to go on. There was still light. Some intuition prodded Cody. Normally he would have spent the night in the shack. Now he was restless. He looked at Walking John. John was tired but game and willing to go. Cody wrapped the cans in his slicker, swung into the saddle and set the horse at the slope above the line camp. By using shortcuts he could be miles along the trail toward San Simon before full dark.

Quelling the rebellion of his empty stomach, he rode on. He was hungry and tired and upset. The fight at the Park and the recollection of that crawling figure filled his mind. Action seemed to be all that satisfied him. As he topped the ridge above the line camp he saw that clouds were hovering close about Rough Mountain and lightning flashed through their gathering mist. For an instant he was tempted to turn back. Still, the trail ahead was easy. Cody shook his head. He would go on.

The short cut Cody took led him back again to Pinery Canyon and in its gloomy depth he lost sight of the clouds. The trail was gradual and the canyon walls closed slowly. Walking John set his own gait and Cody, his mind filled with other matters, paid only automatic attention to his riding. Ahead thunder rumbled with ever increasing volume.

The rain came suddenly. The first hard, big drops hissed down and spatted against the earth, the rider, and the horse. Walking John, stung by the drops, quickened his gait, and Cody, brought back to full awareness, suddenly lifted his head and looked about him. Overhead were storm clouds. About was blackness. He grinned whimsically. His own bull-headedness had brought on his present predicament.

Walking John, knowing that his rider was on the job again, lifted his head and swung it to the right. Cody pulled him back into the trail, reaching back for his slicker as he did so. Again the big horse swung to the right. A lightning flash illuminated the scene momentarily, and appraised of his position by the flash Cody let the horse go. He was below Cochise Head and close under the head there were caves and shelter.

The bay gelding scrambled up the hillside, scrub oak tugging at Cody's stirrups. Again there was a flash of lightning. Following the rumbling thunder Cody heard water trickling and instantly knew where he was. He leaned forward and patted the horse's neck. Walking John stopped short. Cody dismounted and, rein in hand, led the horse along. In another instant he was under an overhang of rock. The storm descended in full fury.

Under the overhang Cody stripped saddle and blanket from the bay. He put them on the ground, hobbled the horse with rope hobbles from a saddle bag, pulled off the bridle and turned the bay loose with a friendly slap.

Walking John, he knew, would not move far. Indeed the horse moved away a few steps and then came the crunch of grass as he cropped the growth beneath the rock ledge. Cody struck a match against a rock wall, and holding it, moved along under the overhang. Within a few steps the wall to his right disappeared and he knew that he had reached the cave.

There was wood in the cave, left by some vagrant of the hills. Cody found it, broke short pieces, curled a stick of cedar into shavings with his knife and shortly a tiny cone of flame showed. With his fire lit, Cody went back for saddle and blankets, brought them into the cave and throwing the blanket over the saddle, set about preparing his meal.

The tomatoes he ate cold. With the can empty he slid it out into the storm and let it rain full. Rinsing it he again caught water and brought his little bag of coffee from his saddle pocket. With the coffee on the blaze and the can of corn set close to the fire to warm, he fell to cleaning the debris and droppings from the cave. Outside the rain settled into a steady downpour, and within the cave the smoke of the fire went up to cling against the roof.

When the coffee had boiled Cody set it off the fire and opening the can of corn with his knife, ate the contents. The coffee settled while he ate, and he drank it with relish, rolling and lighting a cigarette between sips. Having finished his meal he pulled the saddle closer to the fire, and with his back against it and a cigarette between his fingers, sat and contemplated the blaze.

Cody's mind was full of the happenings of the last few days. His talk with Tim Auliffe, his meeting with Clay Stevens and with Bradford, the talk with Pendergast and the happenings of the day, all passed in review. There was little to connect any of these events and yet Cody had the sensation, the uneasy feeling, that each fitted into its respective niche and that the separate parts made a whole.

He had been in the cave almost an hour and the rain had ceased its first mad splatter, when from below he heard Walking John nicker. With the sound Cody came to his feet. His hand went up to his armpit and came out laden with steel, then like a flash he moved into the darkness of the cave away from the fire.

Walking John's shrill whistle was answered and Cody's tension was relieved. An outlaw would not let his horse neigh; still, the visitor did not appear. The sound of hoofs came above the beat of the rain, a horse stopped just at the outer edge of the light from the fire and a rider swung down. The rider came into the fire-lit circle, a rider covered by a yellow pommel slicker. Cody stepped forward, sliding his Colt back into the holster. The rider was Timmy Auliffe.

For an instant the girl and the man faced

each other across the fire; then Cody stepped around the glowing coals and held out his hand. 'I'll tend to your horse,' he offered gravely.

Timmy threw back her head with a defiant gesture. 'No, thanks,' she answered, 'I'll ride on.'

Cody shook his head slowly. 'Not now,' he said gently. 'You're lucky to have found this place. The hills are bad at night in a rain.'

The girl stood stock still for an instant and then suddenly placed her reins in Cody's outstretched hand. 'You'll have to hobble Cry Baby,' she said.

Cody nodded. Methodically he set about stripping off the saddle and blanket. He cut a piece from his own saddle rope and knotted it about the horse's pasterns. When that was done he pulled off the bridle, and the horse, dark with the rain, moved away to join Walking John. Cody, carrying the saddle and gear, came back into the cave.

'I'll make some coffee,' he said tonelessly, and set about rinsing the tomato can and refilling it with water.

Timmy watched him. She had pulled off the slicker she wore and hung it on a rock that jutted from the cave wall. Her hat was placed above the slicker and the firelight caught bright lights in her hair. Timmy spoke suddenly.

'Do you know why I didn't go on?'

Cody said, 'No,' with no questioning inflection in his voice.

'It wasn't because you told me not to.'

Cody made no answer but stared at the fire. The silence hung heavy as the smoke in the cave. Timmy's voice was cold as she spoke.

'I wanted to talk to you,' she answered.

'Yes?' said Cody.

'Do you know what you did the other day? My father hates you!'

Cody's voice was dogged. 'I had to carry out orders.'

'Even when it came to ruining the man who raised you?' Scorn in the girl's voice now.

'Somebody would have brought the word.'

'But why did you bring it?'

'I thought that . . .' Cody stopped. It was useless to explain that he had thought he might be able to soften the blow.

Timmy waited for him to continue. When he did not she took a new tack. 'Big Tim won't tear down his fences,' she said proudly.

Again Cody said nothing. It was useless to reply. There was nothing he could say. The girl, too, was silent for a moment.

'Big Tim is hiring men,' she resumed after a moment's pause. 'He'll fight for what he thinks is right.'

Cody slowly shook his head. 'There's no use, Timmy,' he answered. 'He can't fight the United States.'

'And I suppose you are the United States?'

'No,' slowly, 'I represent the government, that's all.'

Timmy was silent. Cody waited for her to speak and when she did not, suddenly poured out what was in his mind. 'Stop him, Timmy,' he pleaded. 'I know it's hard but it's got to be. I thought that mebbe he'd take it kinder from me than from a stranger. I thought . . . Oh, what's the use?'

The girl's voice was still hard. 'He didn't take it kinder! He says that you're a traitor to him. He says . . .'

'There's no use, Timmy.' Cody's voice was hoarse. 'I'd do everything I could for your father but I can't go back on my oath. I've got to follow this through. I've got to . . .'

The pain in the man's voice reached the girl. She stepped swiftly around the fire and stopped close to Cody's side. Some faint feminine perfume from her hair filled his nostrils and although he did not touch her he could feel her trembling. In that instant Cody Venture knew that he loved Timmy Auliffe.

'You can quit, Cody,' she urged. 'You can resign. I'll tell Big Tim. I'll make him understand. After all the thing that would matter would be in knowing that you are on his side. I've been over to see Lance Blount. Tim sent me over. Lance will take father's side and so will all the other ranchmen. They won't let the fences be torn down. Can't you see, Cody? If you'll quit and join father and the

59

others, all your friends . . .'

A groan was wrung from Venture's tight-set lips. It would be easy to do as the girl suggested, easy to leave this position, which after all meant nothing to him, and join with the men he had known all his life. And Timmy! Her blue eyes, blue-black now, were pleading with him. With every fiber of his body he wanted to reach out and take her in his arms. He knew that if he did take her she would not resist. Tension almost overwhelmed the two in the cave, and then, gradually, Cody relaxed.

'No, Timmy,' he said gently, 'I can't quit now. I've got to go on. I've got to.'

'For me, Cody?' Timmy Auliffe's voice was vibrant.

'Not even for you, Timmy,' Cody said gravely. 'I've said that I would see it through.'

Silence reigned in the cave. Timmy Auliffe stepped back and walked slowly around the fire. Her eyes were big as she stared across the glowing embers. There was a questioning light in those eyes. Cody attempted to answer the question.

'My dad was a marshal,' he said lamely. 'The first one in the territory. He was killed following a thing through. I've . . .'

Sharp and incisive as a knife, the girl's voice cut his words. 'You needn't explain,' she said coldly. 'I think I understand.'

She turned and walked a few steps from the fire. Her action broke the spell that had held

Cody and he moved in turn. From his saddle he took his slicker and the blanket and carried them to a wall where sand lay in a shallow mound. He spread down the blanket, put the slicker over it and gestured toward the meager bed.

'You can lie down here, Timmy,' he said gently. 'Come mornin' I'll take you home.'

The girl looked at him, a long, enigmatic gaze, and then walked toward the pallet he had made. As she approached Cody stepped back. Scornfully she kicked the blanket and slicker aside. Cody stood and watched as she substituted her own saddle blanket and slicker for those she had spurned. When she had settled herself on the thin pallet Cody put fresh wood on the fire from his scanty supply and as it blazed he spoke once more.

'I'm sorry, Timmy.'

The girl made no reply and Cody Venture, retreating to the far side of the cave, sat down with his back against the wall and stared at the flames. How long he sat there he did not know. A movement across the fire aroused his attention. Timmy Auliffe, overcome with weariness, had gone to sleep. Gently then, so as not to disturb her, Cody rose and, gathering the spurned blanket and slicker, covered the still figure. For a moment he stood, looking down at the sleeping girl, and then, cat-footed, retired to the other side of the fire, seated himself and with mechanical fingers began the construction of a cigarette. With the solace of tobacco he relaxed gradually and when the cigarette was done he made himself more comfortable and settled down for a long vigil. But tired muscles and a weary brain had their way; lulled by the steady monotony of the rain, Cody Venture, too, slept.

Bright sunlight, streaming into the cave, awakened him. He sat up and rubbed his eyes. The fire was dead, a little mound of black coals and grey ashes. Across from it was a blanket and a slicker, spread out neatly. Timmy Auliffe, awakening before Cody, had departed silently and alone.

CHAPTER FIVE

Two Trails

Timmy Auliffe, waking with the morning light, found herself covered with a long yellow slicker and a stained Navajo blanket. For an instant she stared wildly about trying to place herself. Then recollection overcame the sleep in her mind and she got up, throwing off the coverings. Across the cave she could see Cody Venture. The man had slumped down against the wall that had supported his back, and his harsh, hawk-like face was strangely softened by sleep. For the instant he resembled the boy that, as a child, Timmy Auliffe had worshiped. In that instant a fierce, possessive tenderness swept over her. Resolutely she put the feeling aside. Wounded pride and perhaps some small spark of vanity took its place. She remembered, flushing hotly, that she had practically offered herself to this sleeping man and that he had rejected her offer.

With her face still suffused with hot blood, she silently collected her riding gear, spread Cody's blanket and slicker on the sand, and then, noiselessly, left the cave. Above, the sun glinted on Cochise Head and down the little draw below the cave Walking John and Cry Baby, her own bright sorrel gelding, lifted their heads at her appearance.

It was easy to catch and saddle Cry Baby. The horse was a pet. With the task finished Timmy splashed water on her face from a rain pool, pulled her hat down firmly and mounting, rode down the draw and across Pinery Canyon.

Across Pinery she followed a trail across a ridge and shortly was dropping into Bonita Canyon. At the foot of Bonita was the Seven Slash.

Big Tim was not at home. Bill Longee, the cook, a crotchety, broken-down cowboy, was in the cookshack making cinnamon rolls, and the odor wafted tantalizingly to Timmy as she rode in. Save for the cook, the Seven Slash was deserted. Timmy went to her room after she had unsaddled. With her toilet made she proceeded to wheedle a breakfast from Longee, and then returned to the house. There she busied herself with straightening her room and putting the place to rights. Housework, however, did not seem satisfying, and presently, at a loose end, restless and not exactly knowing what was the matter with her, she went out to talk with Bill. The cook was not in a talkative mood and presently Timmy flounced away with the announcement that she was going for a ride.

Saddling Cry Baby, Timmy then went back to the cookshack where, despite Longee's black looks and sullen mutterings, she prepared a lunch. With the lunch hung on her saddle she mounted and rode west toward the Seven Slash boundary fence.

Near noon Timmy ate her lunch by a water hole and with her hunger satisfied, stretched out at full length in the sparse shade of a windmill, and, staring up at the cloudless blue sky, reviewed her meeting with Cody Venture.

Her thoughts were not satisfying. Timmy was the spoiled daughter of an indulgent father. She had always had her way. Cody Venture had aided in her spoiling and now the first time she had asked Cody for anything of moment he had refused her. Again the recollection of the previous night's conversation flashed into her mind and she reddened. She hated the silent, dark-faced man, hated him with all her being.

As she lay supine, the creaking of the windmill revolving with the breeze forming a monotonous background to her thoughts, a resolve formed in Timmy's mind. Come what might she was through with Cody and all that he stood for. She hoped that she would never see him again. Timmy Auliffe did not know that when a man fills all a girl's thoughts there is usually something besides hatred in the background.

The resolve made, she sat up and looked over to where Cry Baby grazed contentedly. As she looked the horse threw up his head and a faint sound came to Timmy's ears. It was the sound of a shot. Timmy jumped to her feet. She could not believe that she had heard a shot and yet she did not know what else it could have been. She listened intently for a moment and when the sound was not repeated she walked out from the tank, caught her horse, and mounting, rode on westward, resolved to investigate.

The tank where Timmy had nooned was close to the Seven Slash boundary.

Timmy had ridden barely a mile when she came to a fence. She followed down it, riding slowly, and within a half-mile saw another horseman approaching from the south. Timmy did not recognize the rider at that distance but as they drew nearer she saw that it was Clay Stevens. For an instant she felt inclined to turn

Cry Baby and ride back toward the ranch; then, defiantly, she tossed her head and rode on. There was no reason why she should avoid Clay Stevens or anyone else! The two met at the fence.

Stevens lifted his big hat. He made a handsome picture of a man, sitting his horse easily, hat in hand, his bold face lit with a smile. 'Howdy, Miss Auliffe,' he said. 'Didn't expect to find you over this way.'

There was flattery in Stevens' tone. Timmy who had recently been rebuffed by a man, found solace in the admiration of another, and there was evident admiration in Stevens' eyes. 'I thought I heard a shot,' Timmy told him, 'and I rode over to see what it was.'

For an instant Stevens' face darkened, then the smile came again. 'I didn't hear no shootin',' he said. 'I'd of heard it, too. I been comin' along the fence.'

Timmy had watched the sudden play of color on the man's face. It meant nothing to her. She nodded. 'I suppose I imagined it,' she said. 'Do you ride this fence often?'

Stevens shook his head. 'Not a whole lot,' he answered. 'That's the Seven Slash business. I was just followin' along it.'

The girl looked at the man. Suddenly she asked a question. 'What do you think of the President's order about the fences?'

Stevens appeared to consider. Finally he answered, 'Well, I'm a cowman. I reckon the

66

President ain't. I don't know just what to think about it.'

'You know what will happen to our grass,' began Timmy, not realizing to whom she was talking. 'These Chihuahua cattle will come in on our range the minute the fence is down. They'll starve the heavy . . .' The girl stopped short. She had suddenly recalled that Clay Stevens was a Circle B man and that it was the Circle B cattle that Big Tim Auliffe feared.

Stevens interpreted the pause. 'You don't need to worry none about what you say to me,' he said. 'I'm workin' for Bradford, that's true, but he don't own me.'

'I was just going to say that it was a shame,' Timmy concluded lamely.

Stevens pushed his horse a little closer to the wire. 'Look here,' he began earnestly, 'there ain't no real need for your dad to worry none. You an' me could fix the whole thing up, right here.'

Timmy did not understand the import of Stevens' words. She said so. 'I don't know what you mean.'

'I'm a blunt-spoken man,' said Stevens abruptly. 'I'll tell you just what I mean. If you an' me could get together, your dad would be all right.'

Timmy caught his meaning now. She flushed but before she could speak Stevens continued. 'I've watched you a long time,' he said. 'I've always thought you was just about right. I'm foreman for Bradford an' he takes my word about the cattle. If you'd treat me right your dad wouldn't never know there was a Chihuahua on the range.'

'Treat you right?' Timmy still did not get his full meaning. 'I've always . . .'

'Yeah, treat me right.' There was a leer on Stevens' face and something in his eyes that terrorized Timmy. She half lifted the reins she held in her left hand.

'Why, you . . .' she began angrily.

'You don't need to be so high an' mighty,' Stevens leaned closer to the girl, his body partially over the fence. 'I know about you an' Venture. If you ain't too good to spend a night in the hills with him, you ain't too good for me. What do you say?'

Timmy's answer was a lashing blow of the quirt that dangled from her wrist. The double lashes cut across Stevens' cheek, leaving a livid red welt. With a cry the girl whirled her horse and shoved in the spurs. Cry Baby jumped and then settled down to a dead run. Stevens, furious, set his horse against the fence but the animal refused to move, being wirewise. His face scarlet with fury, the Circle B foreman leaped from his horse, jumped across the wire and ran a few steps after the departing girl. Then realizing the futility of the gesture, he walked slowly back to the fence, climbed over it and mounting his horse again, turned the animal and rode west.

Timmy Auliffe kept Cry Baby stretched out and running. Blinded by her anger, she wanted to get away from the fence, from Stevens, from all the environs of the Circle B. It did not occur to her to question how Stevens knew of her stay in the cave. Nothing occurred to her save the wish to get home, to tell her father of the insult and go with him when he avenged it. Gradually her mind cooled and suddenly she realized that she could not tell Big Tim. There were two reasons: It would precipitate trouble between Big Tim and the Circle B, and Big Tim would not be able to understand why she had stopped in the cave under Cochise Head. With that thought she pulled Cry Baby in from his run. Cry Baby was glad to stop.

By the time these thoughts had come to her Timmy was a full mile from the fence and converging on a wide arroyo. She kicked Cry Baby with the spurs, reined him in when he tried to bolt at the insult, and went on toward the arroyo. As she reached its edge she was startled to see Cody Venture, leaning a little forward on Walking John, come up out of the dry wash. There was no escape for Timmy. She had to meet him.

Cody had been slow to leave the cave. He had made coffee before he saddled and had taken his time in drinking it. The interview with Timmy had upset him. When, finally, he had caught up his horse and prepared to depart there had been other things to slow him down. As he rode down toward Pinery Canyon he saw something that Timmy had not seen. Two shod horses had been before him, no, three shod horses!

The tracks of one he made out as those of Cry Baby. He was familiar with Timmy's horse and had no trouble following those tracks. The other set of tracks he picked up under a pine. Whether they had been made before the rain and sheltered by the pine tree or had been made since the rain he could not say immediately. When he found them in an open spot he knew definitely that they had been made since the rain.

Sign is not easy to follow in the hills. Cody, believing that he knew the identity of the originators of those tracks, followed with the hope of verifying his belief. He was expert at trailing and he followed along steadily but slowly. No man can track rapidly when he must go over rock and sand and through brush. Cody followed the trail until he came to the top of the ridge between Bonita Canyon and Pinery. Here he lost the sign. The two riders had split, one going north and the other on west. Cody followed the westward bound rider for a short distance and then encountered difficulty. Above Bonita Canyon a maze of ryolite formations, fantastic and almost unbelievable, made tracking impossible.

Cody rode back from the Wonderland of Rocks and picked up the trail of the north bound rider. This man, too, had taken advantage of the ryolite and shortly Cody lost his trail. Disgusted with himself and with the impossibility of following, he turned back and again started down toward Bonita Canyon. He was determined, if he could not follow the tracks, at least to visit the Seven Slash. He must know whether or not Timmy had arrived home safely.

Cody found only the cook at the ranch and Longee would not talk. Cody tried to find out when Tim was expected back but got no satisfaction. He did learn that Timmy had arrived at the ranch and his mind at rest on that score, decided he would ride on. He was no less startled than Timmy when, coming up out of the arroyo, he met her face to face.

Walking John stopped. Cry Baby stopped. The two riders stared at each other. Timmy's face was still red-stained and her eyes were wide with fright and anger. Cody saw at once that something was amiss with the girl. He spoke quickly.

'What's the matter, Timmy? What's happened?'

Timmy did not reply. For a long minute she sat silent and motionless, then once again her spurs went in and her quirt lashed down. Cry Baby leaped forward, slid down the arroyo bank, struck the sandy bottom and, staggering to keep his footing, plunged across the wash.

Cody turned Walking John to follow, then

abruptly stopped. He had had one experience with Timmy Auliffe within twenty-four hours. He knew the girl's attitude and he felt that the better course would be to leave her to her own devices. Turning Walking John back, he lifted the horse to a lope.

Walking John was a three-quarters thoroughbred. He was not the ordinary run of grass-fed range horse, for Cody kept his mount in a livery barn in Wilcox and the gelding never lacked for grain. Still, in good condition as the horse was, the last three days of riding had worn him down. He responded to Cody's urging, nevertheless, and swept along over the grass and sand of the valley.

Timmy's tracks were easy to follow. Cody reached the fence, saw that a man had crossed it on foot and then turned back. Cody examined the horse tracks on the other side and then, his face grim, dismounted and kicked down some wire. He led John across, replaced the top wire, and set off, following the tracks that led west.

Cody did not hurry now. The tracks he followed led straight toward the Circle B. Cody wanted to know who was at the other end of those tracks. Whoever it was had caused Timmy Auliffe's grief and fright.

Because he favored his horse, Cody Venture was a good hour behind Clay Stevens when he reached the Circle B. He rode into the yard, dismounted and walked toward the porch.

There was a horse in the yard, a Seven Slash horse, and on the porch Big Tim Auliffe was in earnest conversation with Bradford. So engrossed were the two men that they did not see or hear Cody. Auliffe's words carried to the young deputy marshal.

'It's my ranch,' said Auliffe. 'I've tried to make you see it, Bradford, but I guess I can't.'

Bradford's concise words came sharp. 'No. I can't see it your way, Mr. Auliffe.'

Big Tim arose. 'Then I might as well go,' he said heavily. 'I . . .' He turned, saw Cody below him and stopped his speech short. Bradford, too, saw Cody for the first time. He came toward the steps, his hand half extended.

'Mr. Venture,' he began, 'I'm glad that you came in. I was talking to Mr. Auliffe . . .'

Bradford, like Auliffe, stopped short. Around the corner of the house came Clay Stevens. There was a livid welt on his face and his eyes were black with anger. Cody saw that welt and knew how and by whom it had been made. Like a pit terrier he walked slowly and stiff-legged toward Stevens. His eyes never left the man's face and his left hand held the edge of his vest.

'You yellow pup!' he said slowly.

Stevens stopped, took a step back and his hand went to the waistband of his Levi Strauss overalls and stopped there.

'Go ahead an' pull it,' urged Cody. 'You ain't talkin' to a girl now. Go ahead!'

Slowly, Stevens' face turned white, the red quirt-lash standing out like flame. Gradually his fingers relaxed and he lowered his hand. Cody took two more steps. 'You'll know what I'm talkin' about when I tell you to stay clear,' he rasped. 'I'd kill you now if you made a move. I'll kill you on sight if I hear of you botherin' that girl again!'

Stevens made no answer. On the porch Bradford raised his voice. 'What does this mean?' he snapped. 'Venture, what are you trying to do? You, an officer, coming here and acting like this! I'll have your job for this.'

Cody choked out a single sentence. 'Take it and be damned!'

'What are you doin', Cody?' boomed Tim Auliffe, forgetting for the moment his anger for Cody Venture. 'What does this mean?'

Stevens opened his mouth to speak and then thought better of it. He had been about to accuse Cody and Timmy, and then recollection stopped him. He dared not, for his own sake, mention the fact that he had seen the two in the cave under Cochise Head. His face, which had regained some color, blanched again. Had he mentioned that to Timmy Auliffe? He had!

Cody, still tense, still holding the corner of his vest, stepped back a little so that he could see the men on the porch as well as Stevens. All the repressed fury, all his pent-up animosity, broke from him in a single, virulent sentence.

'It's none of your business!'

The words struck Bradford and Auliffe like so many blows. Auliffe's face turned red, Bradford's white. Auliffe stammered, he could not force out the words. Bradford, his eyes snapping with anger, repeated himself.

'I'll have your job for this.'

Cody, eyes again on Stevens, backed toward Walking John. 'Remember what I said, Stevens,' he warned, his voice toneless now. 'You know I mean it.'

Cody reached the horse, and never taking his eyes from the Circle B foreman, got into the saddle. When he was mounted he turned the horse and with head turned back across his shoulder, watching narrowly, rode toward the gate. With all his will he held himself. Red, murderous fury burned in his brain. If Stevens had moved, if he had lifted his hand, Cody Venture would have turned full in the saddle and killed him.

But Stevens did not move, did not stir a finger. Cody reached the gate and still looking backward, ushed his horse through. From the bunkhouse chimney smoke rose, thin and grey, and a faint odor of burning wood was in the air. These things Cody did not notice nor did the men at the house. They watched the young deputy as he rode slowly along the fence, and when Walking John was masked by the cottonwoods that screened the road, each man released a long, pent-up breath.

CHAPTER SIX

A Cook Is Fired

When Cody was out of sight Tim Auliffe
walked slowly down the steps from the porch.
He had witnessed a scene that he was not
likely to forget. There was a thrill of pride in
the big man. For the time he had forgotten his
own feud with Cody and he gloried in the way
the young deputy. marshal had taken the play.
Now bitter recollection fell upon him. On the
ground he stopped and faced Bradford again.

'There ain't no use of me sayin' the things I
could say,' he announced slowly. 'Ever since I
come here all you've talked to me about is
yore foreman. You know a lot about the East,
Mr. Bradford, but you don't know the West an'
you don't know men. You an' me can't get
together now. Maybe we can later after you
learned somethin'.'

Bradford was angry all the way through. He
was not used to being talked to as Cody had
spoken to him, and he was not used to scenes
of violence. The raw murderous feeling that
had flamed out of Cody Venture's eyes and
through his speech had frightened Bradford,
otherwise he might not have spoken as he now

did.

'I know all about the lies that you and others have circulated about Stevens,' he rasped. 'I knew them and knew that they were lies before I hired him. He acts for me in whatever he does! Furthermore, I don't think that you ignorant hillbillies can teach me anything!'

Big Tim Auliffe had been at the edge of his self-restraint all afternoon. This was too much. He flamed suddenly.

'By God, I'll teach you!' he flared. 'You stand there an' call me a liar an' you take advice from a thievin' rustler. You say my fences have got to come down. If you or yore sneakin' foreman set foot on my place I'll kill you like I would any other coyote! Hear me?'

Completely mad, so angry that he did not hear Bradford begin a reply, Big Tim Auliffe stumped to his horse, untied the animal, and flung himself into the saddle. He did not look back as he rode out the Circle B gate.

Big Tim had some time to cool down as he rode home. A pugnacious man, given to blustering his way through, he had been unable to bluff Bradford. Threats had been of no avail and pleading, when he came to that, had not furthered his purpose. Despite his bluffing and blustering, Big Tim was a fighting man in a tight corner and Bradford might well have listened to his big neighbor.

Tim could not understand the viewpoint of

the Easterner and Bradford couldn't get Tim's. The thing was an impasse, but the cards were all with Bradford. Tim could not see that. He had gone to the Circle B on his way back from San Simon, riding out of his way. In San Simon he had talked with a man or two. Tim had not received the backing he had expected to receive. Save for one or two other ranchers in the country he was the only man who had fenced his range. Tim Auliffe found, oddly enough, that now most of the sentiment was against him.

Riding back to the Seven Slash he thought things over and gradually his first anger abated and settled down into a steady resentment. He considered various angles but always he returned to the one insurmountable fact: The fences that were to come down were his fences! The resentment and hate formed concrete in his mind. Bradford, he felt, was taking advantage, and Cody Venture! . . . Tim could not think straight at all when it came to Cody Venture. He was in no enviable frame of mind when he rode into his own ranch yard and back toward the corrals.

There was no one in sight on the place. Smoke was coming from the cookshack and Cry Baby was in the horse trap, but these were the only visible signs of habitation. Big Tim unsaddled, put his gear in the shed and with every indication of a gathering storm on his face, started toward the house.

As Big Tim rounded the corner of the cookshack, Bill Longee, scrawny, mustache drooping, clad only in undershirt, carpet slippers and a pair of disreputable pants, emerged from the door and heaved away a dishpanful of dirty water. The full contents of the pan struck Big Tim, drenching him from the knees down. For an instant Longee stood, wide-eyed, mouth open, gazing at the disaster he had wrought, and then the storm broke.

Big Tim, spluttering profanity, rushed at the cook, fists swinging. Longee squawked once like a frightened hen and dashed into the cookshack, slamming the door. Big Tim, blind with rage, brought up squarely against that door, his nose bearing the brunt of the meeting. Recoiling from the door he bellowed a curse and returned to the charge. Longee, however, had dropped the bar and Tim's assault was fruitless. For perhaps a minute he raged at the door, inarticulate in his wrath, then regaining his vocabulary if not his senses, he made himself heard.

'Damn you!' roared Big Tim, 'you lousy, dishwashin' . . .' From that point he soared to unprintable heights.

There was no reply from the cookshack, nothing upon which Big Tim could vent his wrath. He kicked the door and hurt his toes. There was a fresh outburst. From it a listener could have gathered that Big Tim wanted his cook's heart and preferred that it be served raw. He stumped off a pace or two, heard the bar rattle and returned to the charge. Longee had just been testing the bar; it was still in place. Big Tim found that out. His voice, ordinarily a roar, leaped to a falsetto.

'Yo're fired!' he shrilled. 'Git out! Yo're fired! You hear me?'

That was the culmination of the fray. Big Tim, turning away from the cookshack, found Timmy at his elbow and allowed himself to be led away. When he had gone there was a long, five minutes' silence, then the door of the cookshack opened cautiously and Bill Longee's long, sad face, with the drooping handle-bar mustachios, peered out. Assured that the coast was clear, the cook opened the door wide and scuttled from it toward the bunkhouse, carpet slippers flapping with his speed. Bill had been fired before but never with such force and violence. He was almost certain that Big Tim Auliffe meant it this time.

Timmy led her father into the house, got him into a chair and brought him a drink. She had experienced tantrums and rages before during her twenty-two years but she had never seen Big Tim just like this. Gradually she calmed him. Presently Big Tim was blowing off through the human safety valve of speech and Timmy believed her battle won.

Big Tim was incoherent for a time but that stage passed. Soon he was pouring out his story and Timmy listened. She learned of her father's disappointment, of the failure in backing that he had encountered, and her heart went out to the big man. She knew how Big Tim felt. Men that he had considered his friends had been lukewarm toward him and Big Tim had almost lost his faith in humanity.

When he told her of his talk with Bradford she sat forward eagerly on her chair. Big Tim had calmed somewhat and he gave a not too prejudiced review of the conference.

'Cody Venture come ridin' in just as I was ready to leave,' said Big Tim. 'He was after Clay Stevens an' after him right. I guess if Stevens had reached for a gun there would of been a killin'.'

Timmy's face blanched and her father looked at her narrowly. Recollection, heretofore blotted out by rage, was rising in his mind.

'Timmy,' he said suddenly, 'Cody was callin' Stevens about a girl. He said, "I'll kill you on sight if I hear of you botherin' that girl again!" What did he mean?'

Timmy had never lied to her father. Now she felt forced to deceive him. She could not tell him of her meeting with Stevens at the fence. Could not tell him about seeing Cody in the cave. She swallowed convulsively.

'I don't know,' she said, shaking her head.

Big Tim refused to believe her. With a stride he was out of his chair and at her side. 'You do too know,' he rasped, shaking her shoulder. 'It was you he was talkin' about!'

Timmy jerked from under her father's hand. She came to her feet, eluded his grasp, and fled. Big Tim, following her, was an instant late. For the second time within thirty minutes he had a door slammed and bolted in his face.

Baffled, Big Tim beat on the door and ordered Timmy to come out. When he received no answer he first tried persuasion and then threats, but Timmy was in no mood or condition to talk to her father and she remained silent. Finally Big Tim gave it up. He stumped out of the house, rounded it and paused.

Before the cookshack stood a two-wheeled cart with a team of little, fat Spanish mules hitched to it. Even as Tim looked, Bill Longee came from the cookshack and carefully deposited a violin case on top of the load in the cart. Cart and mules were Bill's personal and peculiar property. With the violin case in place, Bill stood, one foot on the cart wheel, reached back into a hip pocket and brought out a bottle. Big Tim recognized it as an extract bottle. Bill lifted the container and drank thirstily. Long years of cooking had given him a taste for vanilla extract. As he lowered the bottle he glanced back and his eyes encountered Big Tim's. Longee gave one frightened yelp and leaped to the seat of the cart. A whip whirled out to lash the backs of the startled mules and they jumped ahead.

The cart jerked, rose on one wheel, almost overturning, and then settled to earth again as the mules straightened out for the gate. Dust floated up after it, engulfing Big Tim who now occupied the spot recently held by the cart. High on the seat, lashing the mules, Bill Longee looked back. Then he settled down to steady driving. From what he had seen, from the way Big Tim Auliffe was shaking his fists, there was no doubt about it. The Seven Slash ranch had parted with a mighty good cook.

As Bill Longee left the environs of the Seven Slash, evening closed in. That meant nothing to Bill. The mules were fresh and he would have the wire edge worked down on them by the time it was dark. Also, if he maintained his steady thirst and the supply of vanilla and lemon extract held out, he would be plenty drunk. Bill had felt this coming on for some time.

Being systematic in his drinking he did not take out his bottle every time he felt the urge, but rather did his drinking on the top of a hill. Shortly it seemed to Mr. Longee that every minute rise in the road was a hilltop. His eyes, showing an abnormal amount of white, stared about wildly. Mr. Longee decided that the whole country was a pinnacle, and that called for further drinks.

As many another and better man has done, Bill felt called upon to relieve his feelings. He did this with words, and there being no one else present, he talked to himself.

'Fired!' he muttered bitterly. 'Best damn' cook in the Sulphur Springs Valley an' Tim Auliffe fired me! He'll be sorry! Yo're damn' right he'll be sorry!' Another drink fortified the conviction and Bill threw away the empty bottle and reached back for another. Vanilla and lemon flavoring were going to be scarce on the Seven Slash.

'Best fiddler, too,' resumed Mr. Longee, struggling with the cork. Having, for many years, played for all the dances held in his immediate vicinity, Mr. Longee highly cherished his musical ability. 'Who's goin' to play for 'em now?' he demanded in triumph as the cork came out.

The thought called for a drink and Bill took it, anchoring the lines between his bony knees as he did so. When he reached down again he retrieved only the left-hand line.

Not a whit embarrassed by this fact, really not noticing it, he blithely snapped the blacksnake at the mules which responded with a burst of speed that set the cart rocking. Bill hauled back on the line he held, bending the mules out of the road toward the left. This fact, too, he failed to note.

'Who?' he demanded again. 'Thash what I wan' to know? Who?'

There was another flourish of the whip.

Bill was past the Seven Slash gate, indeed, he was a good quarter of a mile on Circle B range. The mules, filled with plenty of vinegar, bounced along, curving steadily back toward the Seven Slash fence under the pressure of the left-hand line. They looked like bay, oversized jack rabbits and to an onlooker it would have seemed that momentarily the cart was about to overtake them.

Bill, loose jointed, his long neck weaving and forcing his small head to bob like a turkey's, held the seat by some miracle of drunken equilibrium. From feeling sorry for the Seven Slash he fell to commiserating with himself.

'Besh damn' fiddler in worl'',' he announced to the bobbing rumps of the mules. 'Ain't got a job, ain't got . . . *whoa!*'

Bill was too late. The mules charged into a half-hidden arroyo. The cart dropped to the bottom and Bill went over backward, finishing his maneuver by sliding out over the tail gate. Only the fact that the cart was cramped in the arroyo saved Bill from being left afoot. The mules were struggling madly, trying to paw their way up the bank. Drunk as he was and sliding back over his load as he did, Bill knew that no ordinary fright would make the mules act so. He lit with a thud, the violin case slid down in his lap and for a moment he sat straight up on the sand that covered the bottom of the arroyo. It was dusk in the arroyo but still light enough to see well.

Bill, after a moment's reflection, reached

forward to where the bottle he had opened lay on the sand, picked it up, uncorked it and then took a drink. Regaining his voice he said, 'Whoa,' to the mules. He was very mild and the mules paid no attention. Bill said, 'Whoa,' again, raising his voice a little, then lifted the violin case and stared at it foolishly. The mules pawed the bank but not so impetuously as before. Bill felt that he was having some effect on the mules.

'I said, "Whoa,"' he admonished them.

Following the speech he paused. It seemed to Bill as though he had company in the arroyo, that there was some alien presence there. Cautiously he turned his head. Against the further bank of the wash some three feet from his back, he discerned a white blotch. Gradually it resolved into a face, a familiar face. Bill recognized a friend: Burt Randall. Many a time in San Simon and Bowie and Dos Cabezas Burt had bought Bill a drink.

Bill spoke cheerfully. 'Damn' mules run away, Burt.'

Randall made no answer. Bill struggled with his memory. He couldn't remember that Burt Randall had been in the cart with him but— and he clutched the extract bottle—that was often the case. Frequently Bill had been unable to remember. Maybe Burt had been with him and had been hurt.

'You all right, Burt?' Bill asked. 'How about havin' a drink?'

Still no answer. Bill Longee became a little peevish. He shoved the violin case from his lap and then, rising to his knees, picked it up and put it over the tailgate of the cart. With that done, he turned, still on his knees because he felt that he could not trust them if he got to his feet, and with the extract bottle held out, almost touching the white, impassive face, Bill spoke angrily.

'I invited you to have a drink!' Bill Longee snapped. 'You too good to drink with me?'

With his free hand he reached out and touched a shoulder, dark against the arroyo bank. The shoulder was stiff under his hand. Bill thinking that Randall was offering resistance, clutched it and pulled. The body fell stiffly forward from the bank and Bill Longee's horror-stricken eyes stared down at what had once been the back of a man's head. There was nothing there except a mass of blood and hair with a greyish substance oozing from the gaping hole.

For perhaps one minute Bill Longee stared down, and then with a yell that would have shamed a catamount, he came to his feet. With two scrambling steps he reached the seat of the cart; there he leaned down, snatched at the lines that lay along the tongue of the cart, fortunately getting both of them. A pull to the right, another wild screech, and the mules were straightened out. The cart lurched on one wheel, settled to the sand again and with the mules running as only frightened mules can, Bill Longee started up the arroyo. Within fifty feet he found his whip and the mules added to their speed, if that were possible. White as a sheet, Bill settled down to the business of driving. At a low spot in the right-hand bank he swung the mules up and out of the wash and then straightened them out again for the run across country. Bill wanted to get to civilization and he wanted to get there quickly.

Some time after he had left the arroyo and its grisly occupant Bill recalled that he had liquid strength in the back of the cart. The recollection aided him. He stopped the mules, now tired enough to be handled easily, found and uncorked a bottle of lemon extract and drank the whole bottle. Search uncovered three more extract bottles and Bill put them on the seat beside him. By the time two of them had followed the first Bill was no longer afraid, and when the third bottle had gone the way of all good extract, he was not only unafraid but drowsy. A pinpoint of light swam into his field of vision and he turned the mules toward it. It was completely dark now. Bill had no idea where he was and didn't care. The mules took their own gait and Mr. Longee relaxed on the seat and slept.

Cody Venture, rising up from beside the tiny fire of greasewood that he had kindled, watched interestedly as a two-wheeled cart, drawn by a small pair of bay mules, moved into the circle of light. The mules stopped at his command and Cody, walking over to the cart, found Bill Longee sprawled back over his load in a neck-breaking attitude, and dead to the world.

Cody tried to awaken the cook without success. Tired and worn himself, his temper short, he shook Bill vigorously, but Bill simply flopped limply. Cody stepped back and stood in thought for a moment. He had made a dry camp simply because he refused to push his weary horse further. Also, and Cody would not admit this to himself, the events of the day had been too much for him and he had suffered a mental and physical letdown. Now, with Bill Longee on his hands he came to a sudden decision. He went back to his fire and brought his riding gear and loaded it into the already full cart. It was the work of a few minutes to catch Walking John and tie him to the tailgate. Then Cody put out his fire, climbed to the seat and, assuming command of Bill Longee's personal and private property, set out anew for Bowie.

It was a slow trip into town. The mules were good but they could make only four or five miles an hour and Cody could not urge them faster. It was well past midnight when he reached the little town with his load. There was a light in the station and a sleepy cook on duty at the eating house. Cody tried to arouse

Longee, and, failing, turned the mules and Walking John into Summerford's corral behind the livery, stripped the harness from the mules and made a bed in the feed room for Bill. He dumped the former Seven Slash cook unceremoniously on the bed where Mr. Longee promptly began to snore, and then made his way to the station restaurant. When he had finished his meal and paid the cook, Cody sought the depot. The young marshal was not sleepy and he knew that the night operator would like to talk.

The night man greeted Cody when he stepped to the window.

'Come on in, Cody,' he said. 'Door's open. I got a message for you.'

Cody took the yellow sheet the night man gave him. For a while he studied it. The wire was from Pendergast. It informed Cody that the contracts for fence removal had been let and that Bradford was the successful bidder for the area. Very slowly Cody folded the message and thrust it in his hip pocket.

'Jack,' he said suddenly to the night man, 'did you ever hear the old saying, "Lucky at cards, unlucky in love"?'

Jack, the night operator, nodded.

'What can a fellow be lucky at when he has no luck at all?' demanded Cody and turning he stalked out of the office leaving the startled night operator staring after him.

At the very moment that Cody Venture made his erratic query of the night operator at Bowie's depot, a man came from a dark bunkhouse of the Circle B. Noiselessly he moved to the corral, caught a horse that was tied to the fence and led the animal to the saddle shed. In another five minutes he led the saddled animal away from the corrals and, as he walked, a long-handled shovel might have been seen in his hand. Well away from the shed he mounted and rode east.

In the bunkhouse restless sleepers stirred uneasily. It was warm in the bunkhouse although Arizona nights are cool. There had been a fire in the house all afternoon. In the fireplace ashes dropped from a charred log and fell upon a piece of smouldering blanket, smothering the thin fire that ate at its edges.

The rider who stole so stealthily from the Circle B went due east. At a dry wash near the Seven Slash fence he dismounted and led his horse down an embankment. The animal fought and pulled back and when he had the horse in the bottom of the gully the rider tied it to a convenient soapweed. Then, afoot, he walked a short distance further and stopped.

A match flamed in the gully, briefly lighting the darkened mass that had once been the back of Burt Randall's head. The match sputtered out and there followed the irregular rasp of a shovel on sand and rock. This continued for a time and then ceased. There was a thud and the shovel resumed, presently to stop again. Leather creaked and a bit chain jangled faintly, then the black bulk of a man and a horse loomed against the dark sky.

CHAPTER SEVEN

Felipe Comes to Town

Big Tim Auliffe had relieved himself of some of his wrath when he fired Bill Longee. He returned to the house after he had watched the cook depart and again tried to coax Timmy from her room. Not meeting with any success he left the house and went to the corral. There was a saddle horse in the water gap by the corral and Big Tim caught the horse and saddled. He was ready to ride when Johnny Bowen, the Seven Slash bronc-breaker, came in with a lathered pony. Big Tim gave the surprised Johnny curt orders that he should cook supper, and then swung up on his horse and rode north. He went to the north fence, followed it, and by the time he had covered a few miles was sufficiently calmed to think coherently. Determination replaced anger in his mind, and turning his horse he started back to the ranch.

Big Tim ate very little of the supper Bowen had prepared, and after the meal he left his three silent men in the cookshack and went to the house. Again he tried Timmy's door and, finding that it was still locked, went out to the kitchen. There he unearthed a half-gallon jug of whisky and carrying it went back to the front room. He set the whisky beside his chair, pulled the chair around so that it faced Timmy's door, and with a lamp on a table at his elbow, settled down to a night-long vigil. Grey morning found him still there, red-eyed and sullen, a bare half of the whisky left in the jug.

Big Tim could drink an enormous amount of liquor and not show it, but steady drinking for an entire night was more than even he could stand. As the first faint light filtered into the room, dimming the feeble yellow of the lamp, he heard a stir behind Timmy's door. The girl was moving about in her room. Big Tim stared at the door. The fact that he had almost a quart of whisky inside made him irascible and more than a little uncertain. Still he made no movement. Presently the door opened and Timmy came out.

Like her father, Timmy Auliffe had not slept. Her eyes were sunken and her cheeks were pale. She stopped just outside the door and faced her father.

Big Tim stirred in his chair. 'I been waitin',' he said slowly.

93

Timmy had thought things out through the night. Given half an opportunity she would have told her father the whole story. She loved and understood Big Tim but she did not understand him well enough. She was too much like Big Tim for that. Now the words and the timbre of his voice warned her. She drew herself defiantly erect.

'I been waitin',' Big Tim said again.

'For what?' demanded Timmy. She could not see the jug but she knew that Big Tim had been drinking.

'For you to come out. I want to know if that was you that Cody Venture talked about at the Circle B.'

It was on the tip of Timmy's tongue to say that it was. She stopped the words. Something portentous hung in the balance here.

'I think it was.' The liquor did not show in Big Tim's words or voice. Only his red-rimmed eyes showed that he had been drinking. 'I think that you've been havin' truck with Venture. I'm goin' to get it out of you.'

Big Tim tried to rise from his chair. He was unable to get up but Timmy did not know that. Her hand went to her breast. 'My daughter!' rumbled Big Tim. 'Thank God your mother's dead! She'll never know what kind of a little ...'

'Don't!' exclaimed Timmy. 'Don't say that!'

Big Tim sank back in the chair. 'Get out!' he said thickly. 'Get out before I kill you!'

Timmy looked at him for a long instant and then turning fled to her room.

When she had gone Big Tim picked up the jug and drank deeply. The jug gurgled steadily for a full minute and a half. Big Tim set the jug on the floor. Again he attempted to rise. The exertion was more than he could bear. The big drink he had just taken, coupled with the whisky already under his belt, was too much for him. His head sagged forward and he slumped in his chair. When Timmy, a bag in her hand, came from her room, Big Tim had passed out.

Timmy did not know it. Big Tim's eyes were still open and he breathed hoarsely. The girl said, 'Father!' once, her voice trembling, and when no answer came she walked slowly from the room.

There were horses in the corral. Timmy roped out Cry Baby, missing her first five casts. She put a saddle on the horse, tied her bag to the saddle and mounting, rode out of the Seven Slash and headed north toward Bowie.

Cry Baby kept a steady gait and Timmy, paying no attention to her surroundings, lost herself in the easy motion of her horse. Her thoughts were bitter. She had never seen Big Tim act as he was now doing, and she was too young to realize that the reason for his actions was the trouble that had come upon him. Big Tim had faced trouble before this but never grief of just this kind. He was getting old and with Timmy's mother gone and his faith in his daughter shaken, he was unable to throw off the load.

All these things were not in Timmy's thoughts. She remembered only that her father had threatened and accused her, and that she had failed with Cody Venture. This last idea was exceptionally bitter. Timmy began to believe that she had demeaned herself before Cody and with that thought hate filled her mind. She did not realize that to her Cody was all-important, that the reason she thought of him was because he was her obsession.

When she reached Bowie she went directly to Summerford's livery barn, turned her horse over to the hostler there and leaving her grip went on down the street until she came to Summerford's residence. Maria Summerford was her aunt, her mother's sister. Timmy went into the house and followed the odor of baking ginger-bread to the kitchen.

Maria Summerford was a big, capable, wholesome woman. Amazement filled her flour-smeared face when she looked up and saw her visitor. Amazement changed to pity as Timmy, her eyes filled with tears, flung herself into her aunt's arms. Those arms engulfed the slight figure of the girl and Maria Summerford's deep voice comforted her.

'There, honey. Tell me all about it,' crooned Maria, and thus adjured Timmy poured out an incoherent story of the happenings at the

Seven Slash.

Her aunt listened, her broad face growing gradually harder. When Timmy had finished her sob-punctuated recital, the older woman at once took steps to set things aright.

'Now, child,' she commanded, 'don't you think no more of it. You'll take a hot bath an' go right to bed. That's what you'll do. Don't you fret, honey. Everything will be all right.'

Relieved by having poured out her feelings Timmy allowed herself to be coerced. A big tub of hot water in the heated kitchen soothed her body. A big piece of ginger-bread and a glass of milk aided, and Maria Summerford's soothing words comforted her mind. Put to bed, tucked in and fussed over, her tired eyes closed and when she was breathing deeply and evenly Maria Summerford donned her sunbonnet and sallied forth onto the street. Unfortunately for him, Cody Venture was the first person she encountered.

Cody, at a loose end, was sauntering along, heading toward the arroyo at the south end of the little town. It was his intention to go to the arroyo, sit there, and contemplatively, over many cigarettes, think out his course of action. He encountered Mrs. Summerford almost at her gate, and lifting his hat was about to pass by when she hailed him.

'I just heard about you, Cody Venture!' Maria Summerford's wrath descended upon the young deputy out of a clear sky. 'I heard about you an' all I can say is you ought to be ashamed of yourself!'

Before Cody Venture could recover from the shock, before he could frame a question or a word of reply, Maria sailed past him, grand as a square-rigged ship with all canvas set, leaving Cody to stare after her. He watched her as she went on down the street toward the livery stable and when she had entered the door he replaced his hat and resumed his interrupted way toward the arroyo.

Maria did not find her husband at the livery, but when he heard her voice demanding his whereabouts, Summerford came from Bud Jessop's bar. His wife waited until he had crossed the street and then taking his arm firmly in her own escorted him into the feed room of his livery barn. In the sanctity of the feed room she unburdened herself. Summerford listened intently. He knew his wife, knew that she was not given to alarms and excursions, and when she had finished her recital he nodded slowly.

'We'll have to do somethin',' he decided. 'I'll ride out an' see Tim tomorrow. By golly, he's goin' too far with this.'

'An' I'm goin' to give Cody Venture a piece of my mind,' agreed Mrs. Summerford. 'The girl's in love with him. Anybody could see that except a blind fool. It's time he stopped this carousin' around and settled down an' got married.'

Summerford shook his head. He knew his wife but he also knew Cody Venture. 'Don't you talk to Cody,' he said. 'Don't you, Maria. If you do there's no tellin' how much hell you'll let loose.'

When Cal Summerford used exactly that tone his wife knew that it was time to obey. She sniffed, but agreed to follow orders.

'I won't say nothin',' she promised, 'but you'd better saddle up an' go right out to the ranch now. There's no use waiting 'til tomorrow.'

Summerford agreed to that and went into the barn to get his horse, his wife accompanying him. While he saddled she outlined what she thought would be a proper procedure, and when he rode out of town toward the south, Cal Summerford was primed with enough ammunition to sink a bigger ship than Tim Auliffe.

Cody Venture, sifting moodily in the semi-shade of a clump of prickly pear, saw Summerford ride out of town and wondered about the liveryman's destination. He did not dwell long on that question, however, for he had other problems to occupy his mind. Among these were the telegram he had received from Pendergast concerning Bradford's appointment, the trails he had lost as he came down through Bonita Canyon, the fight in Rustlers' Park and his disagreement with Tim Auliffe and Timmy. It was odd, or seemed so to Cody Venture, that his thoughts should always wind up with Timmy Auliffe. He could not quite understand it.

Cal Summerford, in his turn, saw the solitary figure of the young deputy marshal as he rode south. He recognized Cody, just as Cody had recognized him, but he did not turn aside from the trail. He had rather a long ride to make. Summerford planned to reach the Seven Slash that night, spend the evening and what part of the night was necessary to bring Big Tim Auliffe to his senses, and then bring the big man back to Bowie with him in the morning. As he rode he revolved various speeches in his mind and he had his whole method of attack outlined before he reached the Seven Slash. It was unfortunate that he did not get to use that attack: Johnny Bowen met him as he rode into the Seven Slash yard and when Summerford inquired as to Tim Auliffe's whereabouts, Bowen shrugged.

'He lit out a while ago,' the laconic puncher stated. 'Started south.'

'He tell you where he was goin'?' demanded Summerford.

Bowen humped his shoulders again. 'He didn't tell me straight out,' he answered, 'but I know.'

'Where was it?'

Bowen spat a brown streak and looked quizzically at Summerford. 'Tim was drunk,' stated Bowen, 'drunker'n a lord. He headed out of here for Douglas an' from what he said I'd judge that he was after warriors.'

For a long minute Cal Summerford sat his horse, motionless. Then very slowly he dismounted. 'I reckon,' he said thinly, 'that I'll ride back to town.'

Bowen reached out for the bridle reins of Summerford's horse. 'Yeah,' he said dispassionately. 'I'll look after your horse. We'll have somethin' to eat after a while.'

He led the horse away and Summerford stood where the young Seven Slash man had left him. Warriors! That meant that Tim Auliffe had decided to fight, and—here Summerford's shoulders went up sharply—he had gone to the border for recruits. Tough boys along the border. Plenty of them. It might be very nasty. It would be very nasty. Cal Summerford shrugged again. He would have a talk with Cody Venture when he got back to Bowie, a talk with Cody and another with Scott McGuire. Slowly, then, he walked toward the silent ranchhouse.

*   *   *

Cody Venture remained in the arroyo for some time after he saw Summerford pass, and smoked one cigarette after another. He watched a lizard sunning on a rock. It was peaceful in the arroyo and he did not want to leave. Presently, however, the sun, sliding down behind the mountains to the west, warned him of evening and he rose stiffly and started back to town. He passed Summerford's house and glanced at the curtained windows. He wondered why Maria Summerford had spoken to him as she had, and still pondering that question, he came to Bud Jessop's saloon. There were horses along the hitch rail before the adobe building and Cody absently noted the brands. One animal, its back covered with a heavy saddle, slumped on one tired hip. Cody read the brand exposed. It was a THS, a Terrazas horse. The saddle was ornate, a full-stamped, silver-mounted, tapaderos on the stirrups and with a big, round knob for a horn. There was a rawhide riata fastened to the saddle and a rolled coat and blanket behind the cantle. From beneath the right fender a rifle butt protruded, convenient to the rider's hand. Cody took his eyes from the horse and turned to enter the saloon. As he turned a short, stocky, swarthy man came through the door. For a moment they confronted each other, then right hands shot out and gripped.

'Cody!' exclaimed the dark-faced man.

'Felipe!' returned Cody.

For a moment their hands clasped, then the grip relaxed and the swarthy stranger tucked his arm through Cody's. 'Por Dios!' he exclaimed. 'I'm glad to see you, Cody!'

'An' I'm mighty glad to see you, Felipe,'

returned Cody. 'What are you doin' up here? I didn't think Terrazas could get along without you.'

The second he had uttered the words his face darkened and he spoke regretfully. 'I'm sorry, Felipe. I'd forgot . . .'

The swarthy man's face had darkened, too. 'I know you forgot, Cody,' he said. 'I'm come up about Juan.'

Cody tightened his arm, pressing the other's hand against his side. 'I was there, Felipe,' he said. 'Juan . . . Well, it was just one of those things. I'm sure sorry, compadre.'

Felipe de Cespedes, cow-boss for the THS outfit, older brother of Juan de Cespedes, nodded. 'Yo se,' he said.

The two men stood in silence for perhaps a minute, then with a swing of his body Felipe turned Cody toward the door of the saloon. 'Come on,' he said, and his voice was rough. 'We go have a drink.'

Inside, Bud Jessop, big and hairy, served the two and they drank from their small glasses. When the whisky was down Cody looked at Felipe. 'You staying up here?' he asked bluntly.

Felipe nodded. 'For a while,' he answered. 'I hear of Juan going out over the trail an' I think perhaps I had better stop being cow-boss for the Terrazas a while. I'm staying, Cody.'

'You talk to Scott?' Cody was blunt.

Felipe nodded again. 'It is all right with

Scott,' he answered. 'I'm not going loco.'

'I know,' Cody said seriously. 'If I can help you I will, Felipe.'

'Sure,' returned Felipe.

Bud Jessop came down the length of the bar and leaned against it opposite Cody and de Cespedes. 'I hear you're stickin' around, Felipe,' he said.

'For a while.'

Bud toyed with an empty glass, shoved it back and forth for a moment and then looked up so that his eyes caught those of the Terrazas man. 'Well, hell,' he said awkwardly, 'I liked Juan. If you learn anythin', you count me in, will you?'

A smile flashed across de Cespedes' dark face. 'Amigo mio,' he said softly, 'I sure will.'

Jessop, sentiment relieved, shoved out a bottle of whisky and procured a glass from the back bar. 'We'll just take a little snort together,' he said, pouring liquor. 'Here's how.'

The three took their modest libations together and set their glasses back. Bud wiped his lips with the back of his hand, scowled thoughtfully and then grinned.

'Say, Cody,' he said, 'you know what? There's goin' to be a dance.'

Cody smiled faintly. 'A dance?' he said.

'Yeah. Out to Gantry's. Gantry was in this mornin' talkin' about it. The whole damn' town's invited.'

104

'Is that so?'

'Sure. Say, that makes me think: I promised Gantry that I'd git Bill Longee an' Bar Fly to play for him.'

Cody grinned. 'I brought Bill in last night,' he said. 'He was dead to the world. His team come into my camp.'

'Yeah.' Jessop's voice was dry. 'He was in a while ago. I give him a hair of the dog that bit him.'

'Pretty bad, was he?'

'Draggin' the dust. That extract he drinks would down a horse.'

'I've been aiming to see him today,' said Cody. 'I wondered what made him leave the Seven Slash. Have he and Bar Fly already teamed up?'

'Try to keep 'em apart,' snorted Jessop. 'Sure they teamed up. Bar Fly with his accordeen an' Bill with his fiddle, an' both of 'em sots. They couldn't stay apart. I'll tell you why he ain't at the Seven Slash. Big Tim fired him so hard he bounced.'

'Then that was it,' said Cody. 'I wondered.'

'Of all the teams, them two take the cake,' Bud laughed. 'When he's drunk Bill can't remember nothin' that happened while he was sober, an' nothin' that happened while he was drunk when he's sober; an' Bar Fly can't remember nothin'. I guess Scott will have his hands full with them two.'

'Not for long, if I know Scott McGuire,'

Felipe entered the conversation.

'No,' said Bud. 'Scott will throw 'em in, sober 'em up, an' get 'em both jobs. Well, if you see 'em tell 'em I'm lookin' for 'em.'

'And they'll come down and cadge a free drink off you,' said Cody. 'Felipe, I'm going to eat. You coming along?'

Felipe de Cespedes nodded. With a 'So long' to Jessop the two left the bar together. As they strolled down the street, the harsh outlines of the buildings beginning to dim with the coming of evening, Scott McGuire, standing across the street, called to Cody. Venture crossed the street, Felipe waiting for him on the sidewalk. When Cody joined the lanky deputy McGuire went to business at once.

'Felipe's up here lookin' for trouble,' he said abruptly. 'He's on the lookout for Juan's killers.'

Cody nodded. 'Blame him any?' he asked.

McGuire shrugged. 'I don't blame him but he's liable to go off half cocked; then mebbe he'd get hung. I wish you'd sorta dissuade him, Cody.'

'You know Felipe.' It was Cody's turn to shrug. 'Think you can change him any?'

'Naw,' said McGuire disgustedly.

'Felipe's growed up,' suggested Cody. 'If he's man enough to run a wagon for Terrazas he's man enough to look out for himself.'

'Mebbe.' McGuire produced a plug and

scowled at it. 'We got no more line on that express business than we had. Wells Fargo has got a man workin' out of Rodeo, but a lot of good that'll do.'

'They'll start to spend the money by an' by,' comforted Cody. 'When they do we'll get 'em.'

McGuire changed the subject abruptly. 'You didn't do me no favor when you brought in Bill Longee last night,' he complained. 'Him an' Bar Fly are together an' they're sure cocked an' primed. Say, what the hell did Bill see that scared him so?'

'*I* don't know.' Cody looked his astonishment. 'Is he scared?'

'I'll say he is. He jumps sidewise if you say "boo" to him. Trouble is, he don't know neither.'

Cody laughed. 'Let him get drunk enough an' he'll remember it,' he suggested.

'Not in Bowie he won't,' vowed McGuire. 'Go on along, Cody. Felipe's waitin' for you. Keep him out of trouble if you can.'

CHAPTER EIGHT

A Trap Fails

Business called Cody Venture away from Bowie the day following his meeting with Felipe de Cespedes. He left town without again seeing Felipe. For two weeks he was at Wilcox, at Tombstone, and in Phoenix.

Those two weeks were eventful. During that time Tim Auliffe returned from the South and with him came six grim-faced men who took up their quarters at the Seven Slash. They were silent fellows and they avoided Bowie, San Simon, and Dos Cabezas. They did little work, leaving that to the men already at the ranch, but each day they saddled and rode the fences to the west and north. These, being adjacent to the Circle B, were deemed the first line of defense.

With the addition of these warriors a change came over big Tim Auliffe. Once jovial and blustering, he had become quiet and hard. He drank steadily, the liquor seemed to affect him not at all, and he spurned the advances of his former friends. Tim Auliffe had decided that he stood alone, among enemies, and that state of mind, coupled with the liquor, made him bleak and forbidding.

In the meantime there were changes at the Circle B and in Bowie. Scott McGuire, shrewd, fearless and observing, saw Bradford in town and with Bradford he saw Stevens. The Circle B was hiring men, more men than was normally necessary. McGuire took occasion to question Bradford concerning this increase of personnel and was rewarded with the information that Bradford had received the contract for fence removal and was preparing for it.

McGuire said nothing but noted that the men Stevens hired were, for the most part, strangers to Bowie. They came in on the railroad, were met by Stevens or Wig Parsons, and were hauled out to the Circle B. Scott did not like the appearance of things and said so, profanely.

When Cody returned to Bowie the first man he met was the tall deputy, and McGuire lost no time in apprising the young United States Deputy Marshal of the condition of affairs.

Cody listened quietly while Scott outlined what was happening. Then he asked a question. 'You say that he's got about sixteen men at the Circle B?'

McGuire nodded. 'All of that,' he agreed. 'He's hired nine an' there was seven out there. That makes sixteen.'

'An' Stevens has been doin' all the hirin'?'

'All of it.'

Cody mused for a moment. Then he asked another question. 'Who's out there at the Circle B that I know, Scott, besides Burt Randall an' Wig Parsons?'

McGuire shrugged. 'Tony Arpargo an' Tom Beaumont, for two,' McGuire answered. 'Randall ain't there any more.'

Cody's eyebrows shot up. 'No?' he questioned. 'I thought that Burt an' Stevens was thick as two bugs in a blanket.'

'I guess they were,' answered McGuire. 'All

I know is what I heard Jessop say. Bud said that him an' Stevens was talkin' a while back an' Stevens said that Burt had quit.'

Cody frowned. 'You ain't seen Burt?' he asked.

'No,' replied McGuire, 'I ain't.'

'Well,' Cody's thoughts went off at another tangent, 'what's Auliffe doing?'

McGuire grinned, the smile hard and tight. 'Makin' war talk,' he replied, 'an' drinkin' all he can hold. Mebbe more.'

Cody's frown deepened. 'He hired some men,' he said. 'I talked with the deputy from Douglas an' he said that Auliffe had got four or five hard ones from down there.'

'Stevens is gettin' his from New Mexico, mostly,' said McGuire.

'I reckon I better go out that way.' Cody's voice was tired. 'Likely . . .'

'Want me along?' McGuire drawled the words. Cody knew that he had a fighting man behind him. He smiled quickly.

'Not yet, Scott,' he answered. 'I'll handle it for a while. I would like to borrow your glasses though.'

McGuire's face was expressionless. 'I'll get 'em for you,' he said.

When McGuire had departed Cody strolled down toward the post office. He passed Bill Longee on the street, and Bill, looking once in Cody's direction, departed hurriedly. At the post office, just as he was about to enter, Cody encountered Timmy Auliffe.

He stopped short when he saw the girl and then, pulling off his hat, took two quick steps toward her. Timmy, her face white and cold, turned her eyes away and with face averted and with her skirt drawn back as though she were afraid it would touch the man, swept past Cody. For an instant he watched her, then, his eyes bitter, he went on into the post office.

Inquiry brought a letter from the postmaster. Cody, opening it, found that it was from Pendergast and it informed him of Bradford's successful bid, thus confirming the telegram. Cody read the letter through, then with a shrug turned and left the office. Outside the building he met Scott McGuire and the two walked down the street to Summerford's livery.

Cody had left Walking John with Summerford. He did not find the proprietor at the stable and so, paying his bill to the hostler and arranging for a pack horse, he left the stable and went to a store. McGuire waited while Cody ordered provisions, then went back to the stable with the deputy and watched while Cody saddled Walking John and put a pack saddle on the rented horse. When that task was finished McGuire took the big bay gelding and rode out.

'I'll bring you some blankets, Cody,' he said as he rode away. 'You go ahead an' load up.'

Cody nodded. Half an hour later, with

provisions on the pack horse, McGuire's promised bedding lashed over the pack, and McGuire's glasses in a saddle pocket, Cody rode out of town, headed south.

He camped that night on the last low-lying spur of the Dos Cabezas, well south of Bowie. It was dark when he made camp and he turned in without lighting a fire. Morning found him with Scott McGuire's glasses glued to his eyes, watching the corner of the Seven Slash's north fence. It was ten o'clock before his vigilance was rewarded and he saw a rider come along the fence. He watched the man out of sight and then came down from his lookout. Evidently all was as usual on the Seven Slash. Cody did not know, as he lay flat on the ground peering through the glasses, that above him, well up on the spur, another man lay watching and that when Cody came from his post this other, dark-faced fellow also slid down and went to his horses.

Satisfied that the Seven Slash was riding fence and ready for trouble, Cody made a fire, cooked a meal and ate moodily. He wanted to avoid trouble between the Seven Slash and the Circle B. Just how to do it he did not know. Of one thing he was certain and that was that he would have to shift camp to a spot where he could watch the Circle B. Cody wanted to be on deck when the Circle B wagon pulled out to take down fence, but he did not want to go to the ranch. That would smack too much of siding with Bradford and Stevens. He was in a quandary. Thinking the thing over he decided to move camp to a point south of where he was and close to the fence. Some vantage point would present itself, he was sure. Wood, water, and grass for his stock were all that he desired and he was sure that he could find it. Indeed, as he thought, an ideal location came to his mind and at once he set about preparing to move. When he had his pack horse loaded and the saddle on Walking John, he started south, swinging away from the Seven Slash pasture as he rode.

* * *

On the morning that Cody lay on a spur of the Dos Cabezas and watched the Seven Slash fence, Arnold Bradford issued from the Circle B ranchhouse and called Stevens to him. Bradford was brisk as he issued orders and when he had finished Stevens departed with an elated step. The orders for which he had waited had come. This was the day that the Seven Slash fence came down, at least a part of it.

In his turn Stevens issued orders and while Cody Venture was moving camp, a wagon rumbled out of the Circle B, headed toward the west, and with the wagon went the Circle B riders.

Stevens took his entire crew. To make a

good appearance to Bradford he sent some of the regular riders off as though they were on the customary business of the day but these men had orders to meet the wagon at the south end of the fence. Stevens knew that the Seven Slash men were expecting the first move to come either from the north or the east. Accordingly he planned to move against the south fence. Surprise, Clay Stevens believed, in company with a good many famous generals, was the essence of success.

About noon the wagon passed the fence corner and made rendezvous with the other men of the Circle B crew. Stevens had already planned his attack and had chosen his battle ground. Now he marshalled his forces toward it. Half a mile down the fence from the corner the wires dipped through a little sag. On either side rocky knolls swelled. It was here that Stevens chose to stop. There was water in the dip and a good camp site a little further along. The cook drove his wagon to the camping place and stopped. Tools were unloaded, and equipped with shovels, wire-pliers, crow bars, and gloves, the men that Stevens had hired in Bowie and San Simon descended upon the fence. A wrangler gathered wood for the fire at the camp and Stevens, calling his free riders together, made his dispositions.

'You boys,' he directed, 'turn your horses loose on drag ropes an' take rifles an' get up on that hill. You don't need to show yourselves an' if there's anythin' to do I reckon you can 'tend to it.'

There were grim smiles and nods from the group as they scattered, leading their horses away. With his trap set and baited Stevens went down to the fence crew.

'Don't work too hard on that fence,' he directed, 'an' be sure you got all yore *tools* with yuh.'

Again he was answered with hard-faced grins and nods.

For half an hour the men worked lazily. Nothing happened. The cook called the crew in to dinner and in relays they went to eat. It was about two o'clock when Stevens, watching the work, was aroused by a whistle from the knoll to the south. He looked up and back and, seeing nothing, turned his head and again looked toward the north. What he saw set a scowl on his smooth, brown face. Three riders, side by side, were coming from the east Seven Slash fence toward the fence crew. They were inside the pasture and pushing along.

As he looked Stevens made out the center rider. The man on the big horse could be none other than Big Tim Auliffe. Stevens wet his lips nervously. Despite the men hidden on the knoll and the hard-faced gunmen who were working at the fence, Stevens was uneasy. Big Tim Auliffe was a fighter. Still, the showdown was here, the thing he had planned for, and Stevens could not avoid it.

The riders inside the pasture came steadily on. As they drew near, the men at the fence stopped their work and putting aside shovels and bars and pliers, stood, hands on hips, waiting the arrival of the riders. Up on the knoll behind Stevens a rifle clicked and Stevens shook his head. He would not be the aggressor.

At the gap in his pasture fence Big Tim Auliffe reined in. With his hands on his saddle horn he leaned forward, staring at the men in the draw. Perhaps fifteen feet separated Auliffe from Stevens. On either side of the big man his companions, hard-eyed men, sat their horses. One, the man on the left, slipped his foot from the stirrup. Both parties were tense. Neither noticed a man, mounted and leading a pack horse, riding east from the fence corner. This valley between the knolls with its good grass, its wood and running water, had been the camp site that Cody Venture had chosen.

It was Big Tim who spoke first. 'So you dared to do it, Stevens?' he rumbled, deep in his chest. 'You dared to!'

Stevens sought for his voice. When he found it, it was high and shrill. 'I'm here workin' under orders,' he said. 'My boss . . .'

'By God, I'm yore boss!' thundered Auliffe. 'This is my fence yo're tearin' down! Now you can put it back! Every wire, every post, every staple! Understand?'

Stevens had recovered himself now. He was

playing a part and he intended to play it well. 'I'm sorry, Mr. Auliffe,' he said smoothly, and his voice deepened, 'I'm workin' for the government. Mr. Bradford has a contract to pull fences on government land. He sent us down here. You better talk to him.'

Auliffe suddenly lost his temper. 'I'm talkin' to you!' he roared. 'By God . . .'

With his face purple with anger his hand swung back toward his hip, closing on the butt of the gun that rode there. The rider to Auliffe's left dropped from his horse as though shot down, striking the ground and peering under the belly of the animal, a Colt in his hand. The man on Auliffe's right swung his horse away, his hand shooting down for the butt of the carbine in its saddle scabbard.

*   *   *

On the knoll behind Stevens a man rose up, a rifle at his shoulder, and with a thunder of hoofs a big bay horse burst through the men clustered about the fence, and slid to a stop. As Walking John settled to his haunches, Cody Venture, face white and wrath blazing from his eyes, dropped to the ground, leaped between Auliffe and Stevens and halted.

The sudden arrival of the deputy marshal stopped all motion. The man on the hill lowered his rifle and Auliffe's man came from behind his screening horse. For an instant

Cody made no movement, said nothing, then he took two long steps and with his face thrust almost into Stevens' pallid one, he spoke.

'It don't work, Stevens!' he rasped. 'I'm here!'

Stevens recoiled a step from the white-faced deputy. Tim Auliffe, with so much whisky under his belt that his reflexes were slow, did not move as rapidly as his opponent. On him Cody whirled and deluged words.

'You!' he snapped. 'Tim Auliffe! Who do you think you are? God Almighty? Your fence! Your land! Your cattle! You damn' fool! You come riding straight into as pretty a trap as was ever set! In another minute they'd have blasted you off the earth!'

Turning from Tim Auliffe, Cody looked back up the hill. Raising his voice he called once, imperiously. 'You there on the hill! Stand up!'

In answer to that command men rose from behind rocks and yucca; sheepish men, caught in a trick. Auliffe's eyes widened as he saw the full force that he had opposed. A thin, grim smile settled over Cody Venture's lips, but his eyes were rock-hard.

'Tell 'em to go on about their business, Stevens,' he ordered. 'You won't need the army. I'm here an' I'll be stayin' close while your crew pulls fence.'

Auliffe recovered some of his poise. 'They won't touch this fence,' he blustered. 'They won't . . .'

Before the anger of Venture's eyes he quailed and ceased to speak. Cody looked at the big man, a slow, long, smouldering gaze, and then turned back to Stevens.

'You've got a fence crew,' he said pointedly. 'You won't need these riders, I take it.'

Stevens, too, had regained his poise. He scowled at Venture. 'I'm runnin' this!' he began. 'I take orders from Bradford an' he'll tell me what to do. Not you! If you think . . .'

Cody stepped away, wide of Auliffe. Plainly he was restraining himself. 'We can settle this right now,' he drawled. 'You step out away from these men an' I'll step out the other way. One of these fellows can count three. After that you can use your own judgment. How about it?'

Stevens, his face white, hesitated. He was afraid, afraid to take Venture's offer and afraid not to. If he refused the challenge he lost caste with his men. If he accepted it . . . He couldn't accept it. He had once seen Cody Venture's swift and deadly celerity with firearms. He had no wish to be the cause of another such exhibition.

Stevens waited, and as he hesitated a welcome interruption came. Riding down the fence from the corner came another man. As he drew close the men by the gap could see that it was Bradford. The little Circle B owner came on, reined in his horse, and leaning

119

forward in the saddle stared at Stevens and Venture. For a long moment he did not speak. He stared at the men on the ground, lifted his eyes and looked at the men on the hillside, his own riders these; then he glanced at Auliffe. Finally he spoke.

'Stevens,' he said firmly, 'I will not have this! It is too apparent, the thing you meant to do here. You are through! Come to the ranch and I will pay you.'

Stevens, stricken by the sudden words, tried to fight back. 'You can't do that!' he began. 'I'm your foreman. I'm carryin' out your orders. I . . .'

'You are through,' said Bradford firmly. 'All through. Parsons, you will take charge of this crew. Mr. Venture, I will rely on you . . .'

He stopped his sentence. Cody had walked through the men and stood before Bradford. 'I'm here,' he said, his voice hard. 'I'll stay here. This fence will come down and there will be no trouble.'

Bradford bowed slightly. 'Thank you, Mr. Venture,' he said, and without another word, without a glance at Big Tim Auliffe or at Stevens, he reined his horse around and set the animal in motion.

When Bradford had ridden a little distance Cody turned to Auliffe. 'I think you heard me, Tim,' he said. 'I said that I would be here and that there would be no trouble. You and your warriors can go home.'

Tim Auliffe looked at the two men with him. Again he glanced at the rock-strewn hillside that had hidden the jaws of the trap. Then without a word he turned his horse. The two men who rode with him likewise wheeled their mounts, the man who had dropped to the ground, swinging into the saddle again. They, too, rode off, reaching their leader and flanking him on either side. One of them looked back but that was all.

Cody turned to the men at the fence. Wig Parsons, his face a picture of puzzlement, stood at the edge of the group. Stevens was walking slowly toward the wagon. Cody nodded to Wig.

'There's nothin' I can see to keep you from goin' on with the job,' he said slowly. 'Mebbe those boys on the hill have a piece of ridin' to do. They'd better get at it. An' Wig . . . I know all those boys on the hill. They might remember that.'

Wig opened his mouth, closed it again, and then once more opened it to issue orders.

'Get at it!' he commanded. 'Le's get this fence tore down. Hey you fellers!'—this last to the men on the hillside—'you go on back to the ranch.'

Activity at the fence was resumed. On the hillside the Circle B men who had lain in ambush started slowly toward the crest to retrieve the horses which were hidden on the other side. Cody, watching proceedings, laughed suddenly, quick and harsh.

'I'm makin' camp,' he said. 'Remember, I'll be here, Wig.'

Parsons, his face still puzzled, nodded, and Cody, catching up Walking John, rode out after his pack horse. As he returned, riding down the fence again, he saw Clay Stevens, mounted and with a lead horse, leave Wig Parsons and, swinging wide to avoid meeting Cody, start toward the east.

CHAPTER NINE

Charred Evidence

Cody rode to a point well below the Circle B wagon before he stopped. Near scrubby cedars and close by the little trickle of water that the dryness of the country magnified into a creek, he halted, dismounted and began to unpack his horse. As he busied himself with his sparse preparations he now and again looked toward the Circle B wagon which he could see above him.

Cody had just finished unpacking and was hobbling Walking John and the pack horse when he saw the men from the fence come in to the wagon. They were sulky and silent. Cody stood and watched them for a moment and then bent again to the task at hand. When

122

he straightened up he saw that a rider was leaving the wagon, swinging out toward a bunch of horses. The rider picked up the horses and brought them back. Cody watched while the horse herd was thrown into a rope corral and the men with the Circle B crew roped out mounts. He saw the cook harnessing a team. The Circle B was moving. Cody bent down again and took off the hobbles on Walking John.

As he led John over to his saddle he saw the cook mount to the wagon seat and straighten out his team. The other Circle B men were already mounted. Cody threw his saddle up on John's back and watched while the Circle B crew started east. Then he shook his head and reached for a cinch. They were quitting!

There was no need for Cody to stay where he was if the fence crew pulled out. He realized that fact. Leaving Walking John he caught up his pack horse, clamped on the pack saddle and began to repack his outfit. He was filled with curiosity. He wondered why the crew had departed so precipitously. He had an inkling of the reason but he was not sure. He had to know.

When he had finished his packing he mounted and, leading the pack horse, he, too, set out along the fence, riding east.

He had cleared the fence corner and had halted, debating as to whether or not he should ride on to the Circle B, when he saw a rider coming in from the north. This rider spied Cody and lifting his horse to a lope came on apace. Cody waited. As the man drew close Cody could see that it was Felipe de Cespedes.

De Cespedes' brown face was wreathed with a smile as he pulled up and saluted Venture. 'Hallo, Cody,' he said. 'You been doing some riding?'

Cody nodded soberly. 'A little,' he said. 'I aimed to do some more.'

'Then I ride with you,' announced de Cespedes. 'Cody, you are too careless. This morning I watched you from up above when you pulled out. I . . .'

'Why didn't you come into camp?' demanded Cody.

'I was looking for someone.' De Cespedes shook his head.

'So was I,' said Cody. 'I found 'em, too. Say, Felipe, I just run into the damnedest thing.'

'So?' Felipe lifted his eyebrows in interrogation.

'Yeah. Listen.'

He told de Cespedes then of the sudden departure of the Circle B wagon and crew. Felipe listened and when Cody had finished he laughed. 'They work for Stevens,' he said with a shrug. 'I bet you they have all quit now.'

'Mebbe,' said Cody, 'but I want to find out.'

The two friends rode on toward the Circle B. They covered ground steadily without hurrying greatly. Presently the ranch buildings came into view and within a few minutes they were riding into the ranch yard.

The wagon, team still hitched, stood near the house. There were horses grazing near the fence and in the yard, but save for the animals the place was deserted. As Cody and Felipe dismounted Bradford came from the house and started uncertainly toward the team. Cody hailed him and the easterner stopped.

'What happened?' demanded Cody bluntly.

Bradford appeared dazed. He looked at the tall deputy and at the shorter, swarthy man who stood beside him. 'They quit,' he said falteringly. 'Every man of them. I had given Stevens his check and he was in the bunkhouse when they came in. Parsons came to me and told me that they wouldn't work for me. He demanded their pay. I wrote their checks and when I had that done I went out to talk to them. They wouldn't listen. Stevens just laughed at me!'

Cody shrugged and grinned grimly. Felipe de Cespedes laughed. 'See, Cody?' he said. 'I told you.'

'Yeah,' returned Cody, 'they never were workin' for you, Mr. Bradford. They were workin' for Stevens.'

'But why?' said Bradford, uncomprehending.

'You wouldn't understand,' interrupted Venture. 'Felipe, you'd better unharness that team. I'll run those horses into the pasture for you, Mr. Bradford. I reckon we'll stay tonight.'

Felipe walked over to the wagon, climbed to the seat and taking the lines, started the team toward the barn. Cody mounted Walking John and started out after the loose horses. Bradford, amazement still on his face, watched them go.

The Circle B was denuded of men, Cody and Felipe discovered when they had finished their self-appointed tasks and had looked after their own riding stock. Felipe competently took charge of the kitchen while Cody did what chores he could find to do about the yard. Bradford wandered about the place, watching first one and then the other. He could not yet realize just what had happened. Bradford had been playing gentleman rancher. All the work had been done by his men and under Stevens' direction. He had money, and in the East he was able as the next, but here on an Arizona ranch he was helpless. When Felipe called them in to supper Bradford walked in with Venture and the three sat down to the meal. It was odd to see de Cespedes, a flour sack around his waist and the black butt of a heavy Colt peeping over the sacking, flour on his arms and a smudge of it on his face, put hot biscuits, steak, potatoes and canned corn on the table.

When they had eaten a little and the edge was partially taken from their appetites, Bradford loosened his tongue. He had been through a somewhat shocking experience.

Cody and Felipe listening, gathered that Bradford had been treated none too gently by the departing crew. They had not touched him physically, that was true, but the two Western men garnered from Bradford's reticently told story that he had been informed as to his short-comings and that some rough promises had been made him.

Cody, putting down his fork and picking up his coffee cup, grinned across it at the little Circle B owner. 'I reckon, Mr. Bradford,' he said, 'that right here an' now you've been informed. You fell in with a poor bunch to start with an' you're just finding it out.'

Bradford looked up from his plate and stared at Cody. 'I think I have misjudged you, Mr. Venture,' he said. 'I gathered a wrong impression of you from our first meeting and I want to apologize. Perhaps'—and now he spoke more slowly—'I've been wrong about a number of things.'

It was handsomely said. Cody realized that the words cost the little man an effort. It is always hard to confess that one is wrong.

Cody spoke quickly. 'It's just that you didn't know,' he said. 'This is a new country out here, but an awfully old one in some ways. Men kind of get out of their clothes and you get to know 'em. We'll say that you were just misled.'

Bradford shook his head. 'I trusted Stevens,' he said. 'When I saw what he had planned to do today I couldn't believe my eyes. That was

127

murder he had planned and if you hadn't come when you did . . .'

'Pshaw,' interrupted Cody, 'Tim Auliffe is a hardheaded old fool in lots of ways, but he isn't bad, Mr. Bradford. I reckon there might of been some trouble there.' He grinned sheepishly. 'I kind of lost my head for a second,' he confessed.

Bradford studied his plate in silence. Then, suddenly, he raised his head. 'I've taken Stevens' advice about a great many things,' he began. 'Perhaps I've been wrong in that. Perhaps there is some claim of Auliffe's to that land that is justified. I think I'll talk to him. And, Mr. Venture . . .'

'Yes?' said Cody.

'I had better tell you this: I think that I am to be appointed United States Commissioner. I have set certain influences to work. I may as well tell you that I had planned to have you removed from your place. I don't know how you will feel about it. Now, of course, I've learned more than I knew and . . .'

'Shucks,' said Cody, 'forget it.'

Felipe, who had gazed alertly, first at one and then at the other of the two men, now chuckled softly. 'We have a love feast here pretty soon,' he said. 'What are you going to do about all your cows, Mr. Bradford?'

Bradford was not sure. He was still somewhat bewildered. Cody saw an opportunity. Here was a chance to help Scott

128

McGuire and keep Felipe in line.

'Why don't you stay with Mr. Bradford a while, Felipe?' he suggested. 'You don't have a lot to do an' this would be a good place as long as you're in the country.' Turning, he explained to Bradford. 'Felipe here is a THS wagon boss. You couldn't get a better man to help you out.'

Bradford seized eagerly on the suggestion. Felipe was none too willing to fall in with the idea. He wanted to be a free agent but native politeness made refusal almost impossible. Bradford was so eager, so insistent, that Felipe de Cespedes finally capitulated. With a shrug he agreed to stay for a while at the Circle B.

'I'll count on you to hire the men you need,' Bradford said to Felipe. 'I find that I really know nothing about this business.'

Cody watched with an amused smile as Felipe grudgingly accepted the responsibility. Bradford, relieved and glad to relinquish authority, continued to talk. He gave Felipe a brief outline of the status of the Circle B as he knew it, told him about the number and kind of cattle and their approximate disposition.

Cody, listening, grew more and more interested. He interjected a question. 'You brand the D Cross besides the Circle B, Mr. Bradford?'

Bradford looked startled. 'I have just the one brand,' he replied. 'Stevens bought cattle from Mexico, Mr. Venture. Most of them were purchased from the Terrazas ranch. I know of no D Cross brand.'

'There's a heap of D Crosses runnin' with yore cows,' said Cody dryly. 'They got to belong to somebody.'

Felipe, interested, edged forward. 'I see D Cross cows,' he said. 'I wonder about that. What you think, Cody?'

Cody shrugged. 'We can find out who owns 'em,' he replied. 'What are you goin' to do about that fence of Auliffe's, Mr. Bradford?'

Bradford considered for a moment. 'I guess I will go ahead with that,' he announced finally. 'I have the contract. I . . .'

'It's the law that it's got to come down,' agreed Cody. 'Look here, Mr. Bradford, why don't you go over to the Seven Slash and make an agreement with Big Tim? You keep your cattle on your own grass an' him keep his where they belong. After all, there's such a thing as range usage in this country. Your Chihuahuas will ruin Tim if they get on his grass. They'll just starve his heavy stuff to death. Tim's used that country for a long time an' he's improved his stock a lot. You two ought to be able to get together.'

Bradford had been shaken by the events of the day. His eyes reflected his doubts. 'Stevens said . . .' he began.

'You found out several things about Stevens,' suggested Cody.

'I'll think it over,' Bradford spoke slowly.

'I'm beginning to find out a number of things. Perhaps it would be a good idea to have a talk with Mr. Auliffe. It might be that some equable arrangement could be made.'

'Fine,' Cody voiced his approbation. 'Why don't you an' Felipe go in to Bowie in the mornin'? Felipe will want to get some men an' you won't want to stay out here until you get a cook. Stevens even took your Chinaman with him. You go in with Felipe. You can find out about this D Cross business an' you'll learn a heap from Felipe. After all, yo're the owner here. You ought to have the say.'

Bradford nodded decisively. 'I'll do it,' he stated.

Cody got up and stretched. 'I'm goin' to turn in,' he announced, his level voice hiding his triumph. 'You goin' to sleep in the bunkhouse with me, Felipe?'

'I have extra rooms,' offered Bradford. 'You can stay here. You . . .'

Cody wanted Felipe alone. 'We'd be more at home in the bunkhouse,' he stated. 'Let's clean up the kitchen an' turn in.'

When Cody and Felipe had washed and put away the dishes, they went out to the bunkhouse despite Bradford's expostulations. They were barely inside before Felipe voiced his protest.

'I do not want to stay here, Cody,' he objected. 'I am here on business. Juan . . .'

'I'm beginning to think that you couldn't

have a better place,' interrupted the young deputy marshal. 'You can ride out of here all you please. You'll be the boss an' you'll have several men that you can trust that'll help you look an' listen. Besides that you'll be helpin' me out a heap, Felipe. You can work on Bradford an' get him to lookin' right at things. Mebbe you can stop a mighty mean fight.'

Felipe shrugged. 'If you say it that way . . .' he said.

Cody clapped his hand on de Cespedes' broad shoulder. 'I knew you wouldn't fail me,' he commended. 'Come on. Let's strike a light and turn in.'

A match flared in Cody's hand and by its aid he found a lantern on a table. With the lantern shedding a feeble glow in the long room of the bunkhouse Cody threw the still flaming match with which he had lit it into the fireplace, and removing his hat seated himself on a bunk.

'We'll get my blankets in a minute,' he said. 'You dumped my bed in the saddle shed, didn't you?'

Felipe nodded.

Light flamed briefly in the fireplace. 'I better put that out,' said Cody, rising. 'It's hot enough in here without a fire.'

He walked across to the fireplace, set his foot on the flaming paper and then stopped. 'I'll be damned,' said Cody, stooping. 'Wonder who's been burnin' a blanket?'

Straightening, he walked back toward the

table, carrying a small charred fragment of cloth in his hand. By the light of the lantern he examined his find.

'"B.R.,"' he said slowly. 'Stitched in this. I wonder? . . .'

'I theenk you have got me into one hell of a mess, Cody,' announced Felipe. 'I will stay because you are my friend an' you say I can help you out, but I do not like it.'

Cody absently put the charred fragment of blanket into his pocket and sat down again. 'Now listen, Felipe,' he began patiently.

Felipe shrugged, but he, too, sat down. Cody leaned forward, went over his argument again, pointing out the advantages of the position on the Circle B. Felipe listened impassively, rolled a cigarette and was unconvinced. Matters were still in that status when Cody finally gave up, rose, and went out after his bedding.

The three men at the Circle B were up early the next morning. They ate breakfast and when the meal was done Cody ran in horses while Felipe cleaned up the kitchen. Cody saddled for all three, packed his pack horse and was waiting when Arnold Bradford and Felipe came out. The three mounted and leaving the Circle B, rode toward Bowie.

When they had ridden some little distance from the ranch, Bradford spoke to Cody. 'About that fence contract, Mr. Venture,' he said abruptly.

'Yes?' Cody was expectant.

'I'm going to let it go until I can have a talk with Mr. Auliffe,' announced Bradford.

'Good!' Cody voiced his approbation.

'It must come down, you understand that?' Bradford looked at the lean man riding beside him.

'That's the order.' Cody's voice was a slow drawl.

'Still there's no use in precipitating trouble.' Bradford was still watching Cody.

'No,' returned Venture. 'I think you're right, Mr. Bradford.'

Bradford nodded. 'I'll talk with Auliffe and then I'll see you,' he announced. 'I'm beginning to learn how men feel in this country. I had a lesson yesterday.'

'Why, that's fine,' drawled Cody. 'First thing you'll be an Arizonian.' With that doubtful compliment the conversation dropped. The trio rode on silently, Bradford from time to time eyeing Cody interestedly.

It was noon before they reached Bowie. They ate dinner at the railroad restaurant and then separated. Bradford had decided to stay in town, taking a room at the railroad hotel, until there was a crew at the ranch. Felipe de Cespedes, armed with full authority, sallied forth to acquire a crew of riders, and Cody Venture, bidding Bradford goodbye, went out to find Scott McGuire. He wanted to tell McGuire the happenings at the Seven Slash fence and the Circle B ranch, apprise him of the situation. Cody believed, not unreasonably, that there would be more trouble at the Seven Slash and Circle B. Clay Stevens had a crew of men. Stevens was not one to give up easily.

Walking down the street from the depot toward Bud Jessop's Alcatraz Saloon, Cody saw Lester Harp, brand inspector for the district, standing under a wooden awning across the street. Cody stopped and then walked across to where the Stock Association man stood.

He greeted the brand inspector and after a moment's idle conversation, asked a question. 'Who owns a D Cross brand around here, Lester?'

Harp looked at Cody for a moment and then pulled his brand book from his pocket. 'D Cross,' he said. 'I don't remember seein' that, Cody. There ain't been any D Cross cattle shipped out of this district.'

'There's plenty of 'em in it,' replied Cody grimly. 'Somebody must have that brand registered. These here are all THS vented an' a D Cross on the hip. Left ear cropped an' right underbit.'

Harp consulted the brand book. There were one or two new pages, supplements sent out from the Association's office. Presently the brand inspector raised his eyes.

'Says here, D Cross on hip, left crop an' right underbit,' he announced. 'Registered by

Clay Stevens an' Burt Randall.'

Cody grunted as though he had received a body blow. 'Thanks, Lester,' he said quietly.

'Sure,' said Harp. 'Anythin' funny about it, Cody?'

'No,' drawled Cody, 'nothin' funny. So long.' Leaving the brand inspector he went on down toward Jessop's.

Scott McGuire was in the Alcatraz. Cody drew him to one side and with the lanky McGuire listening intently Cody told what had happened and what he had learned. When he finished McGuire gave a soft whistle.

'Nice, huh?' he commented. 'Clay was branchin' out for himself. Got a nice little bunch of cattle runnin' on the boss's grass an' when the boss fires him the whole crew quits. Mighty nice.'

'The hell of it is,' ruminated Cody mildly, 'that I just got Bradford in a mind to talk things over with Tim an' get straightened out. Tim's fences got to come down but I think Bradford will be reasonable an' keep most of his stuff off Tim's grass. Damn it!'

'Clay Stevens won't do nothin' like that,' drawled McGuire. 'He's got all Chihuahuas, too, an' they're all along Tim's fence. I'll give you just one guess what's goin' to happen, Cody.'

'I don't need to guess,' said Cody darkly. 'I know what's goin' to happen.' His face brightened momentarily. 'Stevens will have to

136

have a headquarters,' he said. 'He . . .'

Scott McGuire shook his head. 'Not necessary,' he interrupted. 'He can work a wagon all year long in this country. He . . .'

'He's got to have money, anyhow,' Cody broke in.

'Mebbe he's got it,' suggested McGuire. 'The hell of the kind of jobs we got, Cody, is that we can't do nothin' beforehand. We got to wait 'til the other fellow moves.'

Cody grunted his disgust. McGuire scratched his head. 'Reckon it would do any good for me to hunt up Clay an' have a talk with him?' he asked.

'No,' Cody vetoed the suggestion. 'You're an officer. So am I. All we can do is stand back an' watch. Clay will be in his rights. The land belongs to the government an' he registered the brand, him an' Burt Randall.'

'I wonder where Randall is.' McGuire's voice was querulous. 'I ain't seen him for quite a while. Maybe I could do somethin' with Burt.'

'I don't know,' answered Cody. 'I'm goin' to june along, Scott. Anyhow, you don't have to worry about Felipe for a while. He's hitched.'

'Yeah,' said McGuire. 'Say, Cody, before you go: You goin' to be in town tonight?'

'As far as I know,' answered Cody.

'You can hold things down then,' said McGuire. 'I'm goin' to the dance at Gantry's.'

Cody nodded. 'Go ahead,' he agreed. 'I'll

stay here. I don't want to go out.'

'Good enough,' said McGuire. 'I'll see you before you go.'

With that the two parted.

There was nothing in particular for Cody to do. With no U. S. Commissioner to give him orders he had some time on his hands. He loitered about town and later in the afternoon saw Bradford riding out toward the east in company with several other men. Bradford, seeing Cody, rode over to him and informed the officer that he was going to Gantry's to the dance. The Easterner had never seen a cow-country dance and was quite interested.

Still later in the afternoon Felipe de Cespedes hunted Cody out. Felipe had hired three men to work at the Circle B and was pulling out with one of them immediately. The men de Cespedes had acquired were all natives and were known to Cody. The other two, so Felipe said, would be at the ranch the next day. Cody promised to be in at the Circle B within a day or two, bade Felipe goodbye, and went back to Bud Jessop's.

Bud was not going to the dance. He wanted to but could find no one to run the bar during his absence, so perforce had to stay. Leaving Jessop's Cody went down to Summerford's livery stable. There the hostler told him that Cal Summerford, his wife, and Timmy Auliffe had all left for Gantry's earlier in the afternoon. The hostler profanely expressed his wish that he, too, might have gone. Strolling back up Bowie's main street Cody was impressed with the quiet of the little town. It seemed as though no one were left. He knew that there were people at the depot, in the stores and in Jessop's, but the street was deserted.

Scott McGuire, resplendent in clean shirt, Levis and new hat, met Cody in the Alcatraz Saloon, bought the younger man a drink and turned over the keys of the little jail. Then, he, like the others, left. Cody, moodily rolling poker dice with Jessop, felt an unaccustomed loneliness. He knew that the majority of those who had left would not return until some time the next day. The dance would be an all-night affair with breakfast in the morning. Gantry was known for his hospitality and whenever he had a dance at the ranch the whole country attended. About ten o'clock that night, with Bowie asleep, Cody decided that it was time to call it a day, hunted a room and went to bed.

CHAPTER TEN

Gantry's Dance

Timmy Auliffe had not wanted to go to the dance. Only the insistence of her aunt and her uncle had decided her to put on her party dress and accompany them. However, when she arrived at Gantry's at the foot of the Dos Cabezas, she was glad that she had given in to their importunities. Practically the whole country was at Gantry's and it looked as though Timmy, always popular, were due for a good time.

The Summerfords and Timmy arrived early but there was already a crowd gathered. Mrs. Gantry took the two women into a bedroom in the big house and Gantry drew Cal Summerford aside and refreshed him after his long drive. People continued to arrive. Timmy was surprised to see Arnold Bradford ride in with several men from Bowie. Later on Scott McGuire arrived. Wandering through the crowd Timmy watched for Cody Venture. She did not see him. Cody generally came to the dances unless he was away on business, and Timmy had not given up hope of his arrival. When he did come she determined that she would snub him. There was a good deal of wrath in Timmy's mind, wrath directed toward Cody. However, she did not see the young marshal, nor did she see Clay Stevens.

Bill Longee and Bar Fly, ensconced on a little platform at the end of Gantry's big living room, tuned fiddle and tried a few asthmatic notes from the accordion. Bill not only played but called for the dances and now he raised his cracked voice bidding the formation of sets. Timmy found herself chosen by a boy from the

Three C outfit and was led out on the floor. The music began, a quadrille, and Bill Longee called, 'Salute yore pardners!' Fiddle whining and accordion puffing, the dance began.

The dance had been in full swing for about two hours and Timmy was flushed and breathless, when an interruption came. It was almost ten o'clock. The girl noticed a disturbance at the door and then Big Tim Auliffe, flanked by two of the hard-faced men he had hired in Douglas, entered the room. Gantry hurried over to welcome his neighbor and Timmy, swung by her partner, caught a glimpse of her father's face. Big Tim was red-cheeked and his eyes were puffy, sure signs that he had been drinking. Big Tim was not the only one who had imbibed. The music was fast and furious. Both Bar Fly and Bill Longee had partaken freely of Gantry's hospitality. They were both drunk but that tended only to make the music all the more lively.

At the end of the set Timmy's partner conducted her to where her aunt sat. Timmy sank down beside Maria Summerford and had hardly composed her skirts before the older woman was talking.

'Your father is here,' said Maria. 'Are you going to talk to him, Timmy?'

Timmy shook her head. She knew that Big Tim was not himself and she had not forgotten the happenings of the day she had left the Seven Slash. Her aunt nodded her approbation of Timmy's decision. Sets were forming for the next dance and an eager youngster from Dos Cabezas came to claim Timmy as his partner.

For a time the dance went smoothly. There was a good deal of talk, a great deal of laughter. The Sulphur Springs Valley country was out for a good time and was having it. Then, at perhaps twelve o'clock, the trouble broke.

A schottische had just been finished and Timmy was standing, laughing up into the face of the Dos Cabezas boy, when she heard her father's angry voice.

'I don't want to talk to you, Bradford. The only thing I got to say to you is that you're a dirty, low-lived skunk!'

An instant hush fell on the room and men and women turned. There, just beside the door, Arnold Bradford, his face white, faced Big Tim Auliffe.

Bradford was plainly holding himself in check and trying to keep his temper. The whole room heard his reply. 'I want to talk to you, Auliffe. I think you and I can reach some agreement . . .'

Big Tim interrupted. 'You're a dirty dog, Bradford,' he spat. 'You can't pull that kind of stuff with me.'

If anything, Bradford's face became whiter. 'By God, sir!' he said, 'I've come to you to . . .'

Big Tim's fumbling hand pulled a gun from

142

his waistband. Men don't wear guns at a dance, not in the Sulphur Springs country. Behind Bradford men threw themselves out of line, dragging half-hysterical women into the clear. It was Scott McGuire's harsh voice and Scott McGuire's strong hands that stopped murder.

Scott had worked through the crowd. Fearlessly he threw himself forward, his hands clamping on Tim Auliffe's arm. 'Stop it, Tim!' he rasped. 'You damn' fool. You don't know what you're doin'.'

For a moment the two wrestled. Then other men sprang to McGuire's aid. Big Tim's gun clattered on the floor and the little group of men about him forced him out through the door. Timmy, tears on her cheeks and her eyes filled with terror, fled to her aunt.

'Take me home!' she panted when she reached Maria Summerford. 'Get Uncle Cal and take me home!'

Maria Summerford, patting her niece's shoulder, reassured the girl. 'There, there, dear. Of course we'll take you home. Now where is that Cal Summerford?'

It took time to find Cal. Finally he was produced and immediately acceded to Timmy's wishes. Indeed Timmy was not the only one who wanted to go. Other women and girls, nervous, were seeking their escorts. While the music still played and Bill Longee, his tongue somewhat thick, still called for the sets, the dance was breaking up. Cal Summerford had gone for his team and Timmy and her aunt were waiting near the door, the boy from Dos Cabezas standing nearby.

Timmy put her hand on her aunt's arm. 'Do you think father's all right, Aunt Maria?' she asked. 'Do you? . . .'

Overhearing, the Dos Cabezas boy made answer. 'He's all right, Timmy,' said the Dos Cabezas puncher. 'They got him out in the bunkhouse calmin' him down, an' Bradford's gettin' ready to go.'

Timmy thanked the young puncher with her eyes. Cal Summerford arrived with word that the team and buckboard were ready and after bidding the flustered Gantry and his wife goodbye, the three left.

It seemed as though their going was a signal for an exodus. Party after party approached the Gantrys and awkwardly thanked them for a good time and bade them goodbye. Within half an hour only a few cowboys were left and these, with no partners, did not care to dance with each other. The Gantry dance was finished.

In the meantime Arnold Bradford had departed. He had refused the escort of the men who had accompanied him from Bowie, and mounting his flat English saddle, had set out for town. Bradford was shaken. He had meant to take Auliffe to one side, talk with

144

him and arrive at some agreement which would suit the other man. His peace offer had been spurned. Worse than that, Auliffe had miscalled him and attacked him. Bradford, angry clear through, was in no enviable frame of mind as he rode west.

With Bradford gone, Scott McGuire had turned Tim Auliffe over to the two Seven Slash men. McGuire knew, from long experience, that there was no use in talking to Auliffe inflamed as he was by whisky. Instead he told the Seven Slash men to look after their boss, unloaded Tim's gun and gave it to one of the men, suggesting that they go directly to the ranch and not let Tim out of their sight until he sobered. This the Seven Slash men agreed to do. Leaving them, McGuire walked toward the house.

Lights still flamed in the living room but the dance was finished. Bill Longee and Bar Fly were putting away their musical instruments and Gantry and his wife were beside the door. Gantry was seething in his anger and he expressed himself freely and at length to Scott McGuire. According to Gantry it would be a long cold day in August before Tim Auliffe was welcome at his home again.

While Gantry and McGuire talked Bill Longee and Bar Fly went out. Gantry had already paid them and they had the best half of two quarts of whisky left. They said good night to their employer and to Scott, and went toward the corrals where Gantry punchers would hook up the little mules to the cart if Longee was too drunk to do it himself. The former cook and his slack-mouthed associate had been gone some little time when one of the Seven Slash cowboys appeared.

'You see Tim Auliffe?' he demanded of Scott as he entered the door. 'Curly an' me left him in the bunkhouse while we went to get horses. Somebody'd moved the horses an' when we come back for Tim he was gone.'

'I told you to look after him!' snapped McGuire. 'You fools! Tim's drunk an' he's poison mean. Come on!'

Followed by the alarmed cowboy and by Gantry, the deputy sheriff went through the door and ran toward the bunkhouse.

It was just as the puncher had said. Tim Auliffe was not there and when, after some search, they found the Seven Slash horses, there were only two tied to the corral fence. Drunk or not, Tim Auliffe had found his horse and started out.

It took Scott McGuire only a moment to make his decision. Telling the two Seven Slash men to ride for home and if they found Tim on the way to take him along and keep him until he sobered, Scott got his own horse and after a hasty farewell to Gantry, started back to Bowie. Scott made good time. Too good time. He took a short cut instead of following the road.

While the search for Tim Auliffe was taking place at Gantry's, Bill Longee and Bar Fly were on their way in, riding behind Bill's mules. They were both more than mellow; in fact they were ripe and ready to pick. Three miles and four drinks from Gantry's gate Bill got out his fiddle and Bar Fly unlimbered his accordion. From there on the ride was accompanied by music. The fiddle sounded strangely thin in the night and the accordion seemed not to add a great deal of volume. Nevertheless the two were doing well and enjoying themselves, stopping the music now and again for an occasional drink.

'Know what, Bar Fly?' questioned Bill as the mules traversed a grade and crossed an arroyo. 'I'm beginnin' to 'member someshin'.'

'Huh?' asked Bar Fly, imbibing from his almost depleted bottle.

'I'm drunk, Bar Fly,' said Bill solemnly. 'Almosh as drunk as when I wash shcared. I'm 'memberin'.'

' 'Memberin' what?' muttered Bar Fly.

' 'Memberin' what shcared me,' answered Bill. 'I'm funny that way. 'Member when I'm drunk. Whoa, mules! Got to 'member.'

The mules stopped. Bill took a drink, the last one in his bottle, threw the bottle away and stared toward the stars.

'Shcared,' he said. 'I 'member. I . . . Whoa!'

From the left of the road there came a groan, deep and hollow in the night. The

147

mules shied from the sound. Bar Fly was almost snapped off the cart seat. Bill managed to hold the lines and pull the mules down.

'You hear that, Bar Fly?' he demanded.

'Ghosths!' wailed Bar Fly. 'I'll shee shnakes purty soon. Take me home, Bill!'

Bill Longee was made of sterner stuff than his partner. Thrusting the lines into Bar Fly's unwilling hands he issued orders. 'Hol' these!'

Bar Fly held the lines and Bill climbed painfully from the seat, missing the hub with his foot and falling in a sprawl. He crawled erect and, stumbling, walked in the direction from which the groan had come. After five or six stumbling steps he stopped, fumbled for a match and lit it. The match glared momentarily and went out. Bill took another step, tripped over something soft and sat down. As he tried to regain his balance the groan sounded again, near, right at his feet. Bill found another match and lit it. What he saw partially sobered him. Arnold Bradford was lying in the grass, and as Bill moved Bradford groaned again.

Bill got up. He was drunk but not too drunk to act. He called to Bar Fly and was answered. Bar Fly wanted to go on. He wanted to get away from that place. Bill issued orders and Bar Fly, wrapping the lines around the whip socket, got out of the cart and joined Bill. There was no debate as to what to do. Bill knew what had happened, or thought he knew, which amounted to the same thing.

'Horsh throwed him,' he announced to Bar Fly. 'We got to take him to town. You take his feet.'

Bar Fly obeyed, falling twice before he managed to pick up one of Bradford's legs. Bill was more fortunate. He caught the Easterner's head with his first try and heaved the man up. Bradford was inert, a limp, apparently lifeless, bundle. They carried the man to the cart, dropped him once in their efforts to get him over the tailgate, and succeeding on their second attempt, left the motionless body in the cart bed and went back to the seat. Again several trials were needed but both finally achieved a somewhat unsteady equilibrium on the seat, Bill collected the lines and the docile mules moved along.

It was not due to Bill's guidance that they reached town. The mules followed the road and the road went to Bowie. Nor was it due to Bill's guiding hand that they made fair time. The mules were headed to the barn and knew it. The little cart rattled into Bowie's deserted street, dust puffing up from the mules' feet. Bill pulled back the lines and thundered, 'Whoa!' and the mules stopped, squarely in front of the Alcatraz Saloon in which there were still lights.

Scott McGuire, taking his short cut, had arrived in town before Bill. He had made directly for the Alcatraz, thinking that it would be the logical place to find Tim Auliffe in case Tim had come to Bowie. Scott's arrival had awakened Bud Jessop who had put on a pair of pants and come down from his room above the saloon. They were in the Alcatraz talking when Bill's cart arrived.

Both men came out. Jessop was carrying a lamp.

'Throwed off his horsh,' Bill explained, complacently surveying the officer and the saloon keeper. 'Mush of been drunk. Me an' Bar Fly found him.'

'Who?' snapped McGuire. 'Tim Auliffe?'

'Bradford,' answered Bill. 'Groanin'. Bar Fly thought it wash ghosths.'

McGuire went hurriedly to the back of the cart. Jessop lifted the lamp. For a moment McGuire stood, transfixed, then his voice came sharply: 'He's shot! Here, Bud!'

Jessop hurried to the officer's side, thrusting his lamp into Bill Longee's hands. McGuire had raised Bradford. The back of the cart was blood-soaked.

'My good God!' blurted Jessop.

The lamp trembled in Bill Longee's hands. Bill was drunk, almost drunk enough. The sight of Bradford's pallid, blood-smeared face brought back full recollection.

'He's dead!' screamed Bill Longee, and the lamp fell, to tinkle in the street.

The darkness caused momentary confusion. Jessop and McGuire, however, got Bradford

150

into the Alcatraz and, with another lamp glowing, Jessop went at a run down the street for Doctor Harper while McGuire attended Bradford. Bradford had been shot hard, high in the chest. His pulse was a faint thread, a mere trickle in his wrist, and his breathing was flat and shallow. Harper, arriving half-dressed, shook his head when he saw the condition of his patient, and fell to work at once. McGuire, after watching the doctor for a short time went out to find Longee and Bar Fly.

The two were at the livery stable. Bar Fly had passed out, slumped in a drunken stupor in a corner, but Bill Longee was still able to talk somewhat. He recalled but little of the happenings on his trip to town, and he was too drunk to be coherent.

Cody Venture, wakened by McGuire, joined the deputy sheriff. Cody was aghast at what had happened. He could not but share with McGuire the belief that Tim Auliffe might be implicated in Bradford's shooting. The two officers waited for morning to come before they began their investigation. With the first light they were on the road, out toward Gantry's. Behind them was Bowie, stirred to its depths. There had been killings in Bowie, times when hard cases met and shot and died, but here, if Bradford failed to come out from his coma, was cold-blooded murder. Bowie shuddered and talked.

CHAPTER ELEVEN

Murder?

Cody Venture and Scott McGuire found easily
enough the place where Bill Longee's cart had
stopped. They read the sign about the spot. It
was all there, plainly written in the grama-
grass and the sand. They found where
Bradford's body had lain; saw where he had
fallen from his horse, saw where another rider
had come to the road, met Bradford and
stopped. They trailed this other rider, the trail
leading south and west. The trail reached the
Seven Slash fence and passed through a gate.
Scott and Cody looked significantly at each
other. They continued. At the house they
found the two Seven Slash men who had been
at the dance. These two, Curly Archer and
Rance Davis, were glad to see the officers.
McGuire, his face as though graven from
stone, asked questions.

The Seven Slash men had gone directly to
the ranch from Gantry's. They had arrived just
as morning was breaking. A search had failed
to disclose Tim Auliffe and they were about to
catch up fresh horses and start out when they
had seen Tim riding in.

'I don't know how he got here,' said Curly.
'He was blind drunk. How he ever climbed a

horse an' come through the gate an' all I can't figger. He was here though, so me an' Rance unloaded him and carted him in and put him to bed. He's still sleepin'.'

'Where are the rest of the crew?' asked Cody, curiously.

Curly shrugged. 'The boss let most of 'em go,' he said. 'From what it seemed he was runnin' short of cash an' he couldn't keep no more. Bowen is up at the hill camp an' we're here.'

'Did you give Auliffe back his gun?' rasped McGuire.

The Seven Slash puncher shook his head. 'No,' he replied, 'I still got it.'

'Where's the horse he come in on?'

'We turned it out.'

McGuire nodded. 'I'd like to look at Tim's saddle,' he announced.

'What's the matter?' Rance Davis asked the question.

McGuire looked hard at the speaker. 'You know that Tim an' Bradford had words at the dance last night,' he said slowly.

Both men nodded.

'Well,' continued McGuire, 'Bradford was shot on his way home. He's pretty near dead. We trailed a horse from the place an' the horse come here.'

'Tim was blind drunk, I tell you,' Curly's voice rose a note. 'He couldn't of . . .'

'He got *here*,' said McGuire. 'Let's look at

153

the saddle an' the horse.'

Auliffe's saddle was in the saddle shed. McGuire and Cody examined it. There were saddle pockets behind the cantle and opening these McGuire brought out a pair of fence pliers and a collection of staples. In the other pocket was a gun, a heavy .45. It had been fired once and the smell of powder was still fresh about the muzzle. McGuire looked at Cody and then, slowly, nodded his head.

'I reckon,' he said.

Cody's voice was unwilling as he spoke. 'It looks that way, Scott,' he replied.

They went to the house. Tim Auliffe, half dressed, lay on his bed, snoring. It took a great deal of effort on McGuire's part to rouse him. The two Seven Slash punchers stood by, fright in their eyes. They were hard men, Curly Archer and Rance Davis, hired warriors, but this was just a little too much for them.

With Auliffe awake, his eyes bleared with sleep and drink, McGuire again asked questions.

'Where'd you go when you left the dance last night, Tim?' he snapped.

Tim Auliffe shook his head. 'What dance?' he said.

'Gantry's,' snapped McGuire. 'Where'd you go?'

'I don't remember,' Tim Auliffe tried to lie down again.

McGuire seized his shoulder and shook it.

'You were drunk!' he chided. 'You started trouble with Bradford at Gantry's.'

'Damn his heart.' Bradford's name woke a responsive chord in Auliffe's mind. 'I'll kill that son ...'

'You mebbe got the job done already,' rasped McGuire. 'We found Bradford shot on the road in an' we trailed your horse here. You'll have to come with me, Tim. You're under arrest.'

It was hard to make Tim Auliffe understand what had happened. Hard to acquaint him with the facts. Gradually he wakened and as he did so he sobered. He could not recall the altercation at Gantry's nor could he account for his acts after leaving the place. Fear, cold, deathly fear, began to steal into Tim Auliffe's mind. His big, red face turned pale. He made no expostulations when McGuire ordered him to dress and get ready to go to Bowie.

It was necessary to take a wagon in to town. Auliffe was in no condition to ride. Shaky, frightened, his whole body screaming for liquor, he simply could not sit a horse. Then, too, McGuire wanted to take Auliffe's saddle in. Cody helped the Seven Slash men hook up a team and load the saddle. He watched McGuire, with Auliffe beside him, drive out of the yard gate. When the wagon was gone Cody turned to the Seven Slash punchers.

'It's up to you boys to look after this place,' he told them. 'I'll see that you're paid for doin'

155

it. You get hold of Johnny Bowen an' have him see me.'

Curly nodded, wordlessly.

'I'll go on to town,' announced Cody, and stepped up on Walking John. He followed the wagon out of the yard. It was some distance ahead of him, with Scott McGuire's horse tied to the tailgate. Cody loped his horse and passed the wagon. Then he was struck with an idea and stopped. When Scott and the wagon arrived Cody spoke.

'I don't think I'll go in with you, Scott,' he said casually. 'You don't need help, do you?'

McGuire looked at Auliffe slumped beside him on the seat, and then shook his head. 'I can go on in,' he answered. 'What's on your mind, Cody?'

'Not much,' Cody answered. 'I just got an idea.'

McGuire nodded and clucked to the team. The wagon rolled ahead.

When the wagon was gone Cody struck back toward the trail they had followed to the ranch. When he reached the place where the trail struck the Seven Stash fence, he stopped. It seemed queer to Cody Venture. He knew that a drunk man can often ride a horse when he cannot walk. Still, how could a man as drunk as Auliffe appeared to be, dismount and open a gate and remount? How could he do that when, partially sobered, he could not ride? Cody was puzzled.

The grass inside the gate was tall and matted. Outside it was close-cropped. The Seven Slash was not overstocked. The range outside the Seven Slash fence was overstocked. Cody, leaving Walking John, carefully surveyed the ground around the gate. Coming in, he and Scott had been following a horse trail, and had not made a close examination. Now Cody corrected that error. He saw where a man had opened the gate, dug in his boot heels and pulled against the taut wire. Cody could have sworn that those boot heels were too small to be Auliffe's. There were just those boot tracks, however, and they were partially obliterated by Scott McGuire's where Scott had dismounted to open the gate on the trip in. Cody pushed back his hat and scratched his head. This was queer, and mighty, mighty hard.

He took Walking John through the gate and closed the wire. Mounted, he rode down the fence. A hundred yards below the gate there were horse tracks and more boot tracks. They were fresh, as far as Cody could judge. It was hard country to track in, as far as telling about the freshness of tracks. There were other marks around the spot, boot tracks. These new horse tracks led east, toward the hills. Cody scratched his head again.

He sent Walking John along, following these new, fresh tracks. They paralleled the fence. Where the fence ended the tracks swung sharply to the right. Up there ahead, in the

157

Chiricahuas were the weird ryolite formations. Cody would have made a small bet that the tracks led to them. He shook his head. No use going up there. Reluctantly he turned the gelding and started back.

It was noon before he reached the spot where Bill Longee had found Bradford. Cody searched the place carefully. Bill and the cart and Bar Fly and the mules and Bradford's horse had all combined to obliterate tracks. Hard to find anything. Cody spent a good two hours working over the ground. In the end he had made one discovery. There had been another horse at the place, a horse that did not belong to Scott McGuire and that was neither Bradford's nor Tim Auliffe's nor Walking John; and when that horse had left it had paralleled the trail left by Tim Auliffe! That was all Cody knew. He mounted again and went on toward Bowie.

In Bowie Cody found Scott McGuire was waiting for him. Scott was impatient. He had arranged for a Justice of the Peace court to arraign Tim Auliffe and wanted Cody for a witness. Scott, also, was filled with news. Bradford was still living. He was in one of the two rooms that Doc Harper kept for a hospital and Timmy Auliffe was nursing him.

'Doc said that Bradford stands an even-steven chance,' Scott told the young deputy. 'Timmy heard about Big Tim an' she went right down to Doc's. She's there now. If

Bradford dies it won't be her fault.'

Cody nodded. He could see how Timmy felt, and understand what had prompted the girl's action.

'I got Tim in jail,' said Scott. 'He's sober but he's sure got the willies. He wants a drink mighty bad. He still says that he don't remember nothin' about last night except that he had an argument with Bradford at Gantry's. He remembers that all right.'

Cody nodded his understanding and accompanied Scott down the street to where Bowie's little jail stood. The Justice court was to be in the Alcatraz and the two officers took their prisoner from the cell and conducted him to the saloon.

The hearing was brief enough. As Bradford still lived Tim could not be held for murder. The Justice, however, bound the rancher over to the grand jury on an assault charge and ordered him held without bail until Bradford either died or definitely passed the danger point. Tim, big, bewildered, and frightened at the feeling that was so evidently against him, had very little to say. He could not account for his actions after leaving Gantry's. He remembered finding his horse and starting for home, and that was all.

It was after the hearing, with Tim back in the jail, that Cody told Scott McGuire of his findings when he retraced the trail. Scott listened carefully. When Cody finished, the

159

deputy sheriff shook his head.

'It's kind of far-fetched, Cody,' he said. 'Still there might be somethin'. This horse trail went along beside Tim's?'

Cody nodded. 'Somebody awful smart, Scott,' he said. 'Awful smart an' mighty clever. Somebody that didn't like Bradford an' that hated Tim Auliffe. There's just one man I can figure in those boots.'

McGuire nodded. 'Clay Stevens,' he said. 'He fits. But Clay wasn't at the dance an' we ain't seen him for some time. What are you goin' to do, Cody?'

'Give the calf rope,' said Cody grimly. 'It won't hurt Tim to stay in jail. Mebbe it'll soften him up some. He's been actin' bad. Let him stew an' think it over.'

'Yeah,' McGuire said slowly, 'an' what about Timmy?'

Pain flashed in Cody's face, instantly to be repressed. 'I reckon she'll have to stand it,' he returned.

There was sympathy in Scott McGuire's eyes. 'You think a lot of her, don't you, Cody?' he asked.

Cody nodded wordlessly.

'Well,' McGuire turned his face from his friend, 'good luck, kid!'

Later that afternoon Felipe de Cespedes arrived in Bowie. He hunted for and found Cody. Felipe was excited. Bradford's horse, blood on the saddle, had arrived at the Circle

B. Felipe had come to town to find out what had happened.

Apprised of events by the young marshal, Felipe was silent for a little time. Felipe knew Tim Auliffe but did not particularly like the man. Indeed, Cody was rapidly finding that Auliffe had more enemies than friends in the country. Tim Auliffe's action in fencing the Seven Slash had hurt him with the men that used the open range.

'So,' said Felipe after his moment's thought, 'Tim Auliffe don't be satisfied with what the government says. He shoot Bradford!'

Cody shook his head. 'I don't think so,' he said. 'I think that Tim's a bull-headed fool at times, but he raised me an' he wouldn't commit murder. I know him well enough to know that. No, somebody else shot Bradford. I found horse tracks.'

Cody went on to relate his findings of the morning, Felipe listening carefully.

When he had finished Felipe spoke. 'Me,' said Felipe, 'I don't know. I would have back-tracked that other horse from where you find Bradford an' see where he comes from. I would track further from the Seven Slash fence, too.'

Cody nodded glumly. 'I overlooked some bets all right,' he said. 'We won't be able to do much about it now, though. The wind this afternoon will rub that out.'

'Sure,' Felipe was cheerful. 'Still, you an' me

got ideas, we have. Que no?'

'Yeah,' Cody looked up. 'I got an idea, anyhow.'

'An' me,' said Felipe. 'Now I tell you somethin'. Those cows we got: I know them, some. I'm wagon boss for Terrazas an' some of them cows I have seen.'

'Yeah.' Cody was not particularly interested. He knew that like all good cowmen Felipe could pick out individual cattle and remember some of them for a considerable time. It was not very important, just a part of the cow business.

There was still, however, something for Felipe to say. 'I see yesterday one D Cross cow,' he continued. 'I know that cow for we have trouble with her when we brand. That cow was sold with some in Mejico. Cody, I bet you that cow have never paid duty.'

'Huh?' Cody came fully awake now, snapped out of his lethargy.

'She was delivered in Mejico,' Felipe pursued his idea, 'down below Naco. I look for the other cows, the Circle B, an' I find receipts for duty an' bill of sale. This cow I know I deliver her myself.'

'To whom?' snapped Cody Venture.

'To Burt Randall.' Felipe nodded his satisfaction. 'Sure I remember.'

'Well,' Cody drawled the word, 'what makes you think she come across without payin' duty?'

Felipe shrugged. 'Quien sabe?' he said. 'You call it hunch, Cody.'

'Just good enough to play, too,' grunted Cody. 'I'm goin' to send a wire or two.'

'Seguro.' Felipe looked up from the cigarette he was twisting. 'Me, I'm goin' to see how my boss is this afternoon.'

Cody spent some time at the depot composing his wires. He sent telegrams to Naco, to Douglas, and to Nogales, the closest ports of entry, asking customs officials concerning certain Terrazas cattle imported into Arizona. With that done he ate supper in the railroad restaurant and then went back to town and to the jail.

It was a vastly different Tim Auliffe that Cody saw when he was admitted to the jail. Big Tim seemed shrunken. His cheeks were flabby instead of red and firm, his eyes would not meet Cody's. The young marshal was instantly sorry for the big man. Tim Auliffe had raised Cody and there was a close bond between the two despite their recent differences.

'Had your supper, Tim?' Cody asked, after his first greeting.

Tim shook his head. 'Didn't want any,' he rumbled. 'Cody, I . . .' Tim Auliffe hesitated and then took a fresh start. 'I want to tell you you was right an' I was wrong. I'm into this mess an' there ain't nothin' I can do, but . . .'

'It is kind of bad, Tim,' said Cody. 'Scott tells me you don't remember what happened. I

163

was with him at the ranch and you was still asleep an' . . . '

'I was drunk, Cody,' Tim Auliffe said earnestly. 'I don't remember a whole heap. I know I made a mess of things at Gantry's, an' I kind of recall gettin' my horse an' ridin' out of there, but it's all hazy after that.'

Cody's grey eyes were keen. 'Make a stab at it, Tim,' he urged. 'You got your horse at Gantry's an' you started for Bowie. Remember that?'

Tim Auliffe's shaggy head nodded slowly. 'I remember that,' he said.

'You met Bradford on the road.' Cody pursued the happenings as he had reconstructed them. 'Tim, did you have a gun in your saddle pocket?'

'I don't think so.' Tim was doubtful. 'I had a gun in my pants. I been carryin' one since this trouble came up about the fence . . .' He broke off and eyed Cody uncertainly.

Cody moved his hand impatiently. 'We found a gun in your saddle pocket,' he said sharply. 'It had been shot once.'

'That's what Scott said.' Auliffe's voice was dull.

'Go back to the road, Tim.' Cody was patient. 'Where were you headed when you left Gantry's?'

Auliffe shook his head. 'I don't remember. I wish I could.'

'To town?' Cody was insistent.

164

'It don't seem so.' Tim raised puzzled eyes. 'Seems like I wanted to go home. I had trouble with Timmy, Cody.' Apology in Auliffe's voice.

'Never mind that. You were headed home. Now you met Bradford. He'd turned around to come back to Gantry's, mebbe. What happened, Tim?'

'Seems like I met somebody.' Tim Auliffe was trying to think. 'I can't just recall.'

'Think, Tim!'

Scott McGuire's voice sounded in the jail corridor. Cody got up.

'He's right down here, Timmy,' said Scott McGuire. 'Cody's with him.'

There was a quick patter of feet in the corridor. McGuire appeared at the cell door, a key rasped and the door swung open. In an instant Timmy Auliffe was in her father's arms, her head buried in his big chest, her sobs drowning her words. Very quietly Cody Venture slipped out of the cell and joined Scott McGuire in the corridor. The two walked toward the front of the jail.

'Tough,' said Scott McGuire as they reached the door.

Cody nodded. 'It is,' he agreed. 'Scott, I still think . . .'

'Thinkin' don't prove,' rasped Scoff McGuire.

'But mebbe work will,' returned Cody.

'I wish I'd seen them tracks,' grumbled Scott McGuire. 'I overlooked a bet on that.'

Both men fell silent, and each produced papers and tobacco and rolled cigarettes. In the jail behind them they could hear the murmur of voices: Timmy and Big Tim talking. Cody looked uneasily at McGuire and McGuire returned the glance. Matches flamed and smoke trailed from the officers' lips. The voices ceased. Timmy's feet sounded in the corridor. Scott McGuire turned slowly and walked back to Big Tim's cell.

Cody waited. When Timmy reached the door he spoke. 'Timmy.'

The girl stopped. Her eyes were cool as she surveyed Cody Venture. 'Yes?' she said.

'I'm mighty sorry about this, Timmy,' Cody began awkwardly. 'Mighty sorry. I . . .'

There was no anger in Timmy's voice but the words lashed like a whip at Cody. 'You caused all the trouble,' said the girl. 'My father would be at the Seven Slash today if it weren't for you. I think you are a little late with your sorrow.'

'But . . .' began Cody, leaning forward in his earnestness.

Timmy Auliffe drew away from him. She stepped through the door and Cody drew aside. Without a backward look the girl went down the street. Cody, half-burned cigarette between his fingers, watched her go.

Scott McGuire spoke at his elbow. 'You tell her, Cody?'

Cody shook his head absently. 'She wouldn't

166

listen,' he said listlessly. 'She wouldn't listen to me, Scott.'

Cody did not wait for McGuire's answer. Still holding the cigarette, looking neither to right nor left, he walked away from the jail. Scott McGuire sighed and went back into the building.

Cody went on down the street. His mind was numb. He had intended to tell Timmy Auliffe of the two trails he had seen, to give her some encouragement, some hope. The girl had refused to listen to him. Cody turned into the Alcatraz and at the bar, demanded a drink of Bud Jessop. He was standing at the bar, his glass in his hand, when a man bearing a yellow envelope arrived and after a glance about the room, approached the young deputy.

'Telegram, Venture,' said the arrival. 'The agent asked me to bring it down.'

Cody took the message, proffering casual thanks. Tearing open the envelope he perused the written sheet. It was from Pendergast. Cody's presence was demanded in Wilcox. Business, reflected Cody, went on as usual, regardless of anything that might happen. He would go to Wilcox on the late train.

Leaving the Alcatraz he went back toward the jail. He wanted to talk with Scott McGuire before he left.

CHAPTER TWELVE

Payroll Money

Cody Venture's business in Wilcox held him for several days. There was an accumulation of mail in the United States Commissioner's office. There was one warrant to serve in a civil suit. There were other things to look after. Bradford had been appointed Commissioner but Bradford was in Bowie, hovering between life and death, unconscious, and Cody had no immediate boss.

During those three days Cody received telegrams from McGuire. He had asked the Bowie deputy to keep him posted and McGuire was faithful to his promise. Bradford had not improved, McGuire wired. Timmy Auliffe was nursing him. Nothing had turned up, nothing worth mentioning. McGuire did not advise Cody, in his telegrams, of the fact that he had sought out Timmy Auliffe and talked to her about Cody Venture and Cody's discovery. Scott McGuire was a warm friend of the younger man. He took it upon himself to set Timmy right. Timmy had listened and said nothing and Scott was not sure whether or not he had helped Cody's case.

On his third day in Wilcox Cody received his monthly check. The check came in the late mail and, the bank being closed, Cody was forced to cash it at a store. He took his money, bills for the most part, and stuffed them into his wallet, thanking the merchant for the accommodation. As he left the store and started down the street toward the Commissioner's office he saw a familiar figure step from the door of the Land Office. It was Clay Stevens.

Cody did not hurry his pace but Stevens, apparently seeing Cody, waited for him beside the door. As Cody came abreast Stevens said, 'Venture!'

Cody stopped. 'Well?' he said levelly.

'What are you goin' to do about them fences in the Chiricahuas?' Stevens demanded. 'They come down yet?'

Cody shook his head. 'Not that I know of,' he answered. 'Bradford contracted to pull them an' Bradford isn't able right now.'

Stevens grunted. 'Takin' a damn' long time,' he announced. 'I thought you marshals was in charge of that.'

'We are,' replied Cody. 'You seem mighty interested, Stevens.'

'I am.' There was a hint of triumph in Stevens' voice, a self-satisfied smirk on his face. 'I got a lot of cattle that could use the grass behind those fences.'

Cody's face was blank. 'Cattle?' he drawled.

'D Cross is the brand,' said Stevens. 'I just filed on the head of Bonita Canyon in case you're interested, Venture. I'm goin' to run stuff clear down the west side of the mountains.'

'I see,' Cody drawled. 'Settin' up as a rancher. You branch out sudden, Stevens.'

'I want them fences down!' Stevens was enjoying himself. 'I'm entitled to a share of the grass behind 'em an' I aim to have it. Hear me, Venture?'

'You talk loud enough,' replied Cody. 'I reckon the fences will be pulled in good enough time.'

'By God, they better be!' Stevens blustered. 'I'm goin' to write Washington about it. I'm goin' to write Pendergast, too.'

'I would, if I was you.' Cody kept his temper. 'Anythin' else you got on your mind?'

Stevens was not making the headway he had sought. He wanted to bullyrag the deputy marshal, wanted to make Cody angry. He had not succeeded. He opened his mouth to make further speech, closed it again and shook his head.

Cody nodded. 'I'll see you sometime,' he drawled, his voice expressionless. 'Don't forget to write those letters.'

Turning from Stevens he went on down the street. A little way below the land office he saw Wig Parsons. Wig was standing on the sidewalk. As Cody passed, Parsons turned his back.

There was turmoil in Cody's mind. Clay

170

Stevens a ranchman! Clay Stevens filing on the land at the head of Bonita Canyon, right above the Seven Slash. D Cross cattle in the valley mixed with the Circle B. There wasn't a chance for the Seven Slash.

Cody could not understand it. He knew that Stevens had been a moneyless puncher. He knew that Stevens was in disrepute in the country except with a certain element. He couldn't set up a cow outfit on nothing, yet those D Cross cattle had come from the THS, had been bought and delivered in Mexico. Cody had Felipe de Cespedes' word for that. Where had Stevens got the backing?

Once again at the Commissioner's office Cody sat down in a chair behind the desk, lifted his feet to the desk top and reflectively rolled a cigarette. Mechanically he pulled out his wallet and, opening it, counted the bills inside. Three of them were bright new twenty-dollar notes. Cody looked at that money. It was new, not dirty or wrinkled. He put the bills back in his wallet and pursued his thoughts. Clay Stevens and Wig Parsons!

Cody shook his head. He couldn't get an answer.

Later that evening he received a telegram. The customs men at Naco had answered his query. Duty had been paid on three thousand head of cattle at Naco, three thousand head bought by the Circle B. They had no further knowledge of any cattle crossing the border.

Cody folded the telegram and put it away. He had yet to hear from Douglas and Nogales.

With the work fairly well cleaned up at Wilcox, he was free to return to Bowie. There was nothing further to keep him at headquarters and, anxious to get back, he wired Pendergast that he was leaving Wilcox, and made ready to go. In the morning he took the train east.

When he arrived at Bowie he found that Scott McGuire was out of town. Cody went from the deputy's office directly to Doctor Harper's and there made inquiry concerning Bradford. Harper was more reassuring than he had been.

'He has lost a great deal of blood, Cody,' said Harper. 'He hasn't turned the corner and he is very weak. He has a better chance than he had a week ago, though.'

'Has Scott talked to him?' demanded Cody. 'Have you found out what he knows about who shot him?'

Harper shook his head. 'We haven't dared excite him,' he said. 'He's just about half-conscious. Perhaps in a day or two . . .'

'You let me know when he's able to talk at all, will you?' asked Cody. 'I want . . .'

'Certainly,' agreed Harper. 'If he makes it through it will not be entirely my efforts that have done it. Timmy Auliffe stays beside him almost constantly. The only time she goes out is when she goes to see her father. Bradford

172

just follows her about with his eyes. I tell you that girl just wouldn't let him die!'

'Could I see Timmy a minute?' Cody requested.

Harper nodded and went back into the house. Presently Timmy Auliffe, her face impassive, appeared at the door.

'Well?' she said.

'Timmy, I . . .' began Cody.

The girl looked at the young man standing before her. His troubled face, the grey eyes filled with grief, touched some responsive chord in her mind. 'I can't talk to you now, Cody,' she said.

Was there a tinge of kindness in her voice? Cody was unable to tell. He blurted out what he had to say. 'I'm goin' to clear Tim,' he told her. 'He never shot Bradford. It was somebody else. I got ideas. I'm goin' . . .'

Harper called from inside the house. 'Timmy.' The girl turned. Cody caught at her hand, seized it.

'You got to believe me, Timmy!' he urged hoarsely. 'You . . .'

'I must go now,' said the girl hurriedly. 'I'll talk to you when I can, Cody. Do what you can for Tim.'

She was gone. For an instant Cody stood on the porch of Doctor Harper's home, then turning, his face alight, he walked down the steps and started back toward home, his heart lighter than it had been for weeks.

From Doctor Harper's he went to the Alcatraz. Bud Jessop would have any news that was in circulation. Jessop, however, had very little to tell. While Cody was in the saloon Bill Longee came in and bought a quart of whisky. Bill, apparently, had some money, a thing that in itself was unnatural. After the old man had gone out Cody commented to Jessop on the fact.

Jessop explained Bill's affluence. Tim Auliffe had rehired Bill as cook at the Seven Slash.

'Tim bosses the ranch from jail then?' inquired Cody.

Jessop nodded. 'Johnny Bowen's runnin' the place,' he said. 'He comes in an' goes out.'

Cody said, 'I see.' He wondered if Tim Auliffe had given Bowen orders to remove the fences.

Jessop answered that question without being asked.

'Bein' in jail's had a mighty soberin' effect on Tim,' said Bud. 'He's changed a heap. When he first was throwed in it seemed like all the country was against him. Now there's been some change. Lance Blount come in an' he backed Tim up, right to the hilt. Seems like some more are changin' over too. Tim's give Bowen orders to pull down them fences of his an' now pretty near every man you talk to says what a damn' shame it is that an old-timer like Tim has to lose what he's got.'

174

Cody nodded. 'Is Bowen pullin' the fences?' he asked.

'Not yet he ain't,' answered Bud. 'Leastwise, he hadn't started yesterday.'

'Well,' said Cody, 'a lot can happen in three days. What happened to the boys Tim had at the place?'

'Still there,' answered Jessop.

'An' has Bill parted company with Bar Fly?'

'Not so as you could notice it. They're thick as thieves. Scott swears he's goin' to run Bar Fly out of town but he never gets around to it.'

Cody laughed and pulled out his tobacco. The little cotton sack was empty and with a word to Bud that he would be back Cody left the place and went across the street to a general store.

When he had purchased his tobacco he found that he had no change and proffered a bill from his wallet. It was one of the new twenty-dollar notes. Abe Meyers, the storekeeper, took the money back to his till. Presently he returned, still carrying the note in his hand.

'Where did you get this, Cody?' asked Meyers, looking curiously at the young marshal.

'In Wilcox,' said Cody readily. 'I cashed my pay check there. Why, ain't it good?'

'Good enough,' said Meyers. 'There's somethin' funny about it, though. I checked the serial number with the list we got on the

175

Douglas payroll money. This bill is one of 'em.'

'What?' Cody snapped the word.

'It's part of the Douglas payroll money,' reiterated Meyers.

Cody produced his purse again and took the bills from it. 'By gosh, Meyers, this is funny.'

He accompanied the little merchant back to the office and there, with the list of serial numbers from the Douglas payroll in his hand checked the bills in the wallet. Three of the bills had numbers corresponding to those on the list. When he finished Cody looked at Meyers.

'Don't say a thing about this,' he warned. 'I've got to go to Wilcox and see who paid this out. I know where I got it and it ought to be easy enough to do.'

Meyers promised silence, Cody paid for his tobacco with another old bill, pocketed his change and went out. As he walked down the street back toward the Alcatraz, puzzling over the recent development, an idea struck him, full-fledged, and he stopped short.

The bills he had came from Wilcox. He had seen Clay Stevens in Wilcox. Stevens had been affluent, if appearances meant anything, Stevens was starting an outfit. Stevens had a lot of D Cross cattle. Clay Stevens . . . Cody frowned. He was jumping to conclusions. Better go slow. Better take the regular order of procedure. Go to Wilcox, find out who had paid for goods with those bills. Track the thing out step by step. Cody went on down to the Alcatraz. As he approached the saloon he saw Bill Longee come out the door. Bill was carrying another bottle.

In the Alcatraz, talking again with Bud Jessop, Cody decided to wait for Scott McGuire. He wanted to talk things over with the older man. Really the payroll robbery came in McGuire's province. Cody decided to wait until Scott returned.

Later in the afternoon, while Cody was killing time near the blacksmith shop, he saw Mrs. Summerford coming hurriedly toward him. Maria Summerford was angry, it showed in her walk and her expression. Cody rose as she arrived.

Maria wasted no time on preliminaries. 'Where's Scott McGuire?' she demanded.

Cody shook his head; he didn't know. 'Can I do anything?' he asked.

'You'll have to.' Mrs. Summerford scowled. 'That Bill Longee and that drunken sot they call Bar Fly are down by Doc Harper's an' they got a fiddle an' accordeen. They're makin' the day miserable. You better stop it.'

Cody promised that he would, and hurried off after the lady.

As Maria Summerford had said, he found Bar Fly and Bill Longee close to the hospital, sitting in the shade of a palo verde, indulging in what they fondly believed to be close harmony with violin and accordion. Both were drunk, just drunk enough to argue, and Cody, threatening to put them both in jail, jerked them to their feet and started them up the street. With that done he turned to leave but saw Timmy Auliffe at one of the windows of Harper's house. The girl beckoned to him and Cody hurried toward the house.

Timmy met him at the door. The girl was filled with repressed excitement, so stirred that she could hardly talk coherently.

'Mr. Bradford has just been talking to Doctor Harper,' she said, her voice low. 'Oh, Cody, I know father didn't shoot him!'

'What does he say?' snapped Cody. 'Can I see him?'

'Not yet. Doctor Harper won't let anyone in to see him for a while. He says he turned back to see father again that night. He started back to Gantry's. He didn't meet father. Mr. Bradford says that he doesn't remember seeing father at all. He was riding toward Gantry's and he heard a horse coming up. He stopped. He says that he saw the horse but he couldn't see the rider's face. He remembers that the man fired a shot at him and that he fell from his horse, and that's all. It couldn't have been Big Tim!'

'He didn't see the rider?' Cody had caught the contagion of Timmy's eagerness. 'He didn't see his face?'

'No, but he did say that he was sure it wasn't

father!'

'Huh!' Cody jerked out the ejaculation. 'Sure, is he?'

'Yes.'

'Don't build too much on it, Timmy,' warned Cody. 'He's a sick man an' . . .'

'But his mind is just as clear. I was in the room when they were talking, Cody. He kept looking past Doctor Harper at me.'

'Hmmmmm.' Cody's eyes left the eager face of the girl. He almost shook his head. He could see what Bradford was doing. The Eastern man liked Timmy. Cody had Harper's word for that. Bradford was trying to shield the girl's father and through him the girl.

'It will clear Big Tim,' Timmy said earnestly.

Cody nodded. 'There's some other things that will help,' he said carefully. 'I found a trail that ran beside Big Tim's to the ranch. I . . .'

'Scott McGuire told me about that,' interrupted Timmy.

'He did?' Cody looked his surprise.

'Yes, Scott said . . .' Timmy stopped and blushed. Cody, staring at his boots, did not notice the sudden rush of color. Scott McGuire had bluntly told Timmy Auliffe that Cody loved her and that she was treating him like a dog.

'There's lots of funny things happening,' drawled Cody, talking more to himself than to Timmy. 'Some of the payroll money has turned up. Clay Stevens . . .' He stopped short,

179

recalling where he was and what he was saying. Timmy Auliffe's eyes were suddenly bright. She, too, had recalled something.

'I've got to go in, Cody,' said the girl.

Cody nodded. 'I reckon,' he said lifelessly. 'Just keep stickin', Timmy. This talk of Bradford's will help an' we're workin', Scott an' me.'

Timmy turned. She took a step in through the door and then stopped, turning again. 'I know you had to do what you did, Cody,' she said softly. Then, before Cody could move, the door closed.

Cody went back down town. He should have been thinking of other things, of the payroll money and of Tim Auliffe. Instead he was thinking of Timmy's last words and the tone in which they were spoken. Cody's face was expressionless but his mind was in the clouds.

As he passed the Alcatraz he was recalled to the present. Bud Jessop, with some profanity, was putting Bill Longee out of the door. Bar Fly was already in the street.

'You goin' to do anythin' about this, Cody?' demanded the perspiring Jessop. 'These two sons are makin' damn' nuisances of themselves. You better put 'em in the jug.'

Cody grinned. 'They got their liquor here, Bud,' he observed mildly. 'Seems to me like you ought to stand for 'em a little.' Cody walked on, leaving Jessop swearing and staring after him.

At the jail Cody stopped. He went in, asked the jailor to let him see Tim Auliffe, and was escorted by the man to Tim's cell. When Cody was inside the jailor departed. Big Tim had risen as Cody entered. His appearance was much better than when Cody had last seen him. Abstinence and the fact that once again men were rallying about him had helped Tim. Cody walked over, sat down on the bunk, and spoke.

'It doesn't look so bad, Tim,' he said. 'Bradford talked to Doc Harper. He says that it wasn't you that shot him.'

Big Tim sat down. His shoulders sagged suddenly and his face worked as he controlled his emotions. After a moment he found his voice.

'Thanks, Cody,' he said.

Cody nodded, his face averted from the old rancher. Cody's own emotions were pretty close to the surface. There was a close bond of friendship between the two men.

'Who did Bradford say done it?' asked Tim after a moment.

'He don't know,' answered Cody. 'Tim, you was where Bradford was shot, all right. Scott an' me trailed you straight to the ranch from there, but somebody else was there, too. Somebody was with you, about a hundred yards away, and opened the gate for you and let you in to the Seven Slash. I followed the trail.'

Big Tim drew an incredulous breath. 'You sure of that, Cody?' he demanded.

'Sure,' said Cody. 'After he let you in the gate he closed it and then headed back into the hills.'

'Did you trail him there?'

Cody shook his head. 'I missed several things,' he said wearily. 'I didn't back-trail from where Bradford was shot and I didn't go on from the fence. I overlooked my hand twice.'

Tim Auliffe sat down on the bunk. 'When can I get out of here?' he demanded.

Cody shook his head. 'I don't know,' he answered frankly. 'I don't know, Tim. There's a lot to be done yet.' He paused and thought for a moment, then faced the big man.

'Tim,' said Cody Venture, 'I think this hangs on one man. If you are out of here he'll mebbe get suspicious. With you in jail he may make a break that we can use. Are you willin' to stay here for a while an' side us?'

It was a hard thing to ask. A harder thing to answer. Big Tim Auliffe took a deep breath. 'You're not sure, Cody?' he asked softly.

'Not sure,' agreed Cody. 'We might clear you with what Bradford has said and that trail I found; we might not. Remember, Scott found a gun that had been used in your saddle pocket, an' we trailed you straight to the ranch. A jury might think that Bradford was out of his head. I want it clear, Tim. Clear and clean. If you stay here you'll mebbe help catch a murderer.'

Big Tim Auliffe nodded his grey head. 'I've stood it a while, Cody,' he said slowly. 'I'll stand it a while longer. I want it clear an' clean, too.'

Cody got up from the bunk. Tim, too, arose. Cody called the jailor to let him out and as the man came down the corridor Big Tim's hand descended on Cody's shoulder and Big Tim's voice boomed.

'Stay with it, kid,' said Big Tim.

On the way to the door Cody stumbled over a rough spot in the corridor. Cody was not seeing very well. It had been a long time since Big Tim Auliffe had slapped him on the back and boomed, 'Stay with it, kid!'

CHAPTER THIRTEEN

Bill Longee's Memory

It was late that night before Scott McGuire came in. Scott had been north, toward the Peloncillos, investigating rustling. He had accomplished nothing and as a result he was tired, short-tempered and irascible. Cody was waiting at the one-room adobe that Scott called home, when the deputy sheriff arrived. He unsaddled and put McGuire's horse away while Scott cleaned up and ate a bite of supper. The meal over, Cody outlined his latest findings to McGuire.

'It looks mighty queer,' Cody told him. 'Here's Clay Stevens with a cow ranch an' money when a couple of months ago he was a broke puncher. Here's me gettin' some of that Douglas money in Wilcox. I don't know as I told you, Scott, but the time we had that fight in Rustlers' Park I run onto two trails after we'd split up. They went into the rocks up above Bonita an' I lost 'em. There's a heap of things that point one way.'

'You told me about the trails,' answered McGuire, sucking meditatively on a cigarette. 'Go on an' do your thinkin' out loud, Cody. I'll put in a chip whenever I want to ante.'

'Well,' drawled Cody, 'here's Burt Randall receivin' cattle down in Mexico, Circle B cattle. I got a wire from Naco an' the customs has no record of anythin' but three thousand head of Circle B. Where did the D Cross come from?'

'I don't know,' answered McGuire.

'Neither do I. Burt an' Stevens was thick as thieves. Where's Burt? He's just left the country but before he went he burnt his bedding.'

'Burnt his beddin'?'

'Yeah.' Cody fished in a hip pocket and pulled out a charred piece of wool. Passing it over he continued. 'Felipe and I found that in

184

the fireplace at the Circle B bunkhouse the night that Stevens an' all his crew quit Bradford. Kind of queer, ain't it?'

McGuire examined the piece of cloth. 'Hmmmm,' he said.

'Now I'd like to find Burt,' pursued Cody. 'He received cattle from the THS down below Naco. I'd like to know if these D Crosses paid duty.'

'And if they didn't?'

'It would be some help. Remember, Tim's fences got to come down. The Chihuahuas outside will take the grass away from Tim's cattle like it was greased.'

'An' if they hadn't paid duty then they'd be impounded an' held by the government until the duty was straightened up. I see,' mused McGuire.

'It would help Tim's grass,' offered Cody.

'It would,' agreed McGuire. 'That's sort of by the way, though, ain't it? What about the rest?'

'Well'—Cody's drawl slowed—'there's a heap of the rest. There's Bradford bein' shot after a quarrel with Tim. There's tracks we found to the Seven Slash. There's the gate that was opened for Tim to go through. There's the gun in Auliffe's saddle pocket. There's Stevens takin' up a homestead above Bonita Canyon an' figurin' to run cows all along the Chiricahuas. There's Stevens with an ambush for Auliffe at the fence. Damn it, Scott! I can't help but think it all hooks together.'

'Mebbe it does,' said Scott McGuire, meditatively. 'But where are you goin' to break in, Cody? You got nothin' definite to hook on to. Where you goin' to start?'

Cody dropped his dead cigarette. 'I thought,' he said slowly, 'that I'd start at the beginnin'.'

'An' where's that?'

'Some place above Bonita Canyon,' Cody replied decisively. 'That's where the Douglas payroll went, I'm dead sure.'

'You figure then,' drawled McGuire, 'that it's Clay Stevens. You think that he was behind the payroll robbery. You think that he's the man that shot Bradford. You think he's usin' that payroll money to stake him in his ranch. You don't like Stevens, Cody.'

'No,' agreed Cody. 'Do you?'

'I don't,' McGuire answered, frankly. 'You might be right about the payroll an' him bein' in on that. I don't know. But about Bradford I got some other ideas. Tim Auliffe an' Bradford were at outs over this fence business. They had a fight. We find Bradford shot an' a plain trail to the Seven Slash. We find Tim drunk, not able to say where he was, an' a gun that had been shot in his saddle pocket. It looks mighty like Tim to me.'

'You're forgettin' the other trail an' that Bradford says it wasn't Tim.'

'Bradford is mighty weak. He might be out

of his head an' he might be protectin' somebody.'

'I'll agree to that,' Cody nodded. 'I thought of that, too. Just the same, I can't see it that way. I want to find Burt Randall.'

'An' where you goin' to look for him?'

'Some place in the rocks above Bonita,' answered Cody. 'I'm goin' up tomorrow.'

'An' I'm just damn fool enough to go with you,' answered McGuire. 'You go on to bed, Cody. I'm tired an' I want to turn in.'

Cody nodded, got up and retrieved his hat. 'I'll see you in the mornin', Scott,' he said.

Cody went back to the room he had taken at the hotel, undressed and turned in. For a while he lay awake, thinking things over, trying definitely to substantiate the hunch he had. There was a wealth of facts to work on, but those facts ended in a blank wall. Cody finally pillowed his head on his arm and slept.

While Cody Venture and Scott McGuire talked and considered ways and means in Bowie, two other conversations took place. One was between Maria Summerford and her niece. Maria took Timmy to task. The girl, worn out by her duties in Bradford's sick room, was pale and wan. Maria said so.

'You look like a drowned rat, Timmy,' announced Maria, frankly. 'You got to get out more. You've worked and fretted about all this until you're just a shadow.'

Timmy nodded. 'I've been in quite a while,'

she agreed. 'I'll go to the ranch tomorrow, Aunt Maria.'

Maria Summerford sniffed. 'You ought to stay out there,' she said. 'You have no business tyin' yourself down in a hospital.'

'I couldn't let Mr. Bradford die,' Timmy said slowly. 'I couldn't. People think that Tim shot him. If he died . . .'

Maria walked across and put her arm over Timmy's shoulders. 'He isn't goin' to die,' she comforted. 'He'll be all right and so will Big Tim. You go on to bed now, dearie. You're worn out.'

The other conversation was at the Seven Slash. It lay between Bill Longee and his friend and co-worker, Bar Fly. After his expulsion from Bud Jessop's saloon, Bill had collected the groceries he had come to Bowie to buy, loaded them in his two-wheeled cart, and urging Bar Fly to accompany him, finally got his inebriated friend in with the load. Bill drove grandly out of town, got the mules straightened out for the Seven Slash and lolled comfortably in the seat.

The two were late getting to the ranch. Supper was over and Johnny Bowen, Curly Archer and Rance Davis were more than a little wroth with the cook. To avoid trouble Bill turned the mules into the corral without unhitching, and he and Bar Fly sought the shelter of the cookshack. Johnny Bowen, swearing that he'd be damned if he would do the cook's work, left the mules as they were. With the other two punchers he went to the bunkhouse, after promising Bill various and sundry punishment in the morning. From behind his barred door Bill listened and made uncomplimentary noises.

Johnny and the other two had been gone for some time before Bill unbarred the door. It was hot in the cookshack and the heat had put Bar Fly to sleep. Bill, made of sterner stuff, kept awake and drank a little extract. When he opened the door the night air cooled off the shack and Bill felt the need of conversation. He shook Bar Fly awake.

'Le's play some music,' suggested Bill while Bar Fly rubbed his eyes. 'You got your accordeen?'

Bar Fly didn't have the instrument.

'Well,' said Bill agreeably, 'le's sing.'

He tried a note or two, found that Bar Fly had gone back to sleep, and ceased vocalizing long enough to shake the man awake again.

'You're drunk,' said Bill sternly. 'Drunken bum, Bar Fly.'

Bar Fly, used to such appellations, paid no attention.

'I'm goin' to take you home,' announced Bill, seized by a drunken vagary. 'Drunken bum. Got no business at the Seven Slash.'

He fortified himself with a drink of vanilla. Bar Fly nodded in the corner. Bill, firm in his belief that he was doing the right thing, went out of the door carrying a lantern. The mules were in the corral, still hitched to the cart. Bill opened the gate and led them out and to the cookshack. The ranch hands had unloaded the cart and the bed was empty.

It was necessary for Bill to awaken Bar Fly again. This he did with some labor. After he had Bar Fly awake he took several more drinks. He shared his bottle with Bar Fly and got that individual to a state where he could get to the cart with some aid. Taking a pint of extract with him for emergency use, Bill climbed to the cart seat and started the mules.

Now, with wheels rolling under him, Bill was struck by another notion. The Circle B needed a cook. Bill knew that. He knew that the Circle B crew had quit and that Felipo de Cespedes and three others were holding down the ranch. Drunkenly, Bill resolved to be a good samaritan. Here was Bar Fly. Bar Fly could cook; Bill himself had taught him. What could be more reasonable, more friendly to all concerned, than to take Bar Fly to the Circle B and thus give Bar Fly a job and the ranch a cook? It was a good idea. Bill started the mules west, toward the Circle B.

The night was moonlit. The cacti and the tall grass sent long shadows sloping to the west. The shadow of the cart and mules was gigantic. Bill Longee opened the Seven Slash gate in the west fence while Bar Fly snored on the cart seat.

Bill left the gate down. He drove on, the wheels turning softly on the sod and sand. Occasionally Bill reinforced himself The vanilla in the bottle lowered. Gradually Bill was reaching the point of intoxication he had achieved on the day Tim Auliffe fired him. The tired mules walked steadily along. Bar Fly, unable to maintain his balance, toppled from the cart seat into the bed and Bill let him lie there.

Bill had forgotten his original idea now. It was simply a pleasant, moonlit night and Bill was taking a ride. He pulled in the mules, consulted his bottle, and sat on the seat, staring around. Something was working in Bill's mind. Gradually the alcohol that he had just taken, worked up to Bill Longee's brain. Just at the edge of recollection, Bill looked back. Bar Fly lay in the cart bed, the moonlight striking his pallid face. To Bill it recalled another face. Burt Randall! Burt Randall, dead in a draw with the back of his head shot away. Bill screamed. The mules sprang forward under the lash of the blacksnake and Bill's scream. Like frightened rabbits they stretched to the ground, making time. Bill clung to the cart seat, riding that rocking, lurching vehicle. The road stretched straight to the Circle B and the mules held to it.

Felipe de Cespedes, asleep in the Circle B bunkhouse, was awakened by the arrival of the cart. Bill was still yelling, so hoarse now that

191

his voice was almost a whisper. The mules ran into the corral fence and stopped, throwing Bill back into the cart with Bar Fly. When Felipe and his men, guns in their hands, piled out of the bunkhouse, Bill was lying there, still trying to yell, and the mules were standing heaving, their heads down.

It took Felipe some time to come to the root of the matter. Bill Longee, Felipe was convinced, had the delirium tremens. He pulled Bill from the cart, uncovering Bar Fly who still slept. Bill was chattering hoarsely of Burt Randall, of Burt Randall, dead.

'His brains oozin' out!' screamed Bill, and fought against the hands that restrained him.

It was all confused to Felipe. They carried Bill to the bunkhouse, lit a lantern and tried to quiet him. Bill would not quiet. He chattered of an arroyo. Of Burt Randall, dead in that arroyo. Of being fired from the Seven Slash. Of how sorry Tim Auliffe would be. Of his prowess as a fiddler. It was all confused.

Felipe, resourceful, produced a quart of tequila as a last resort. He gave Bill a big slug from the bottle, and then another. Bill quieted under the effect of the drink. He was over the edge now, beyond recollection. Restrained by Felipe and the three men Felipe had hired, Bill ceased threshing on the bunk, gradually quieted, and finally slept, his mouth open and the fumes of alcohol pouring from it.

Felipe saw dawn. Bill Longee had really

seen something, Felipe was convinced. He remembered that Cody had found a piece of blanket in the fireplace when he and Cody had first come to the ranch. He remembered that there had been the initials, 'B.R.,' on that blanket. Felipe scratched his head and reached a decision. Bill Longee might be seeing snakes but in the morning he, Felipe de Cespedes, would take a look around. He would examine the arroyos close to the Circle B.

Felipe adhered to his program. The four men comprising the Circle B crew ate breakfast at four o'clock. They did not disturb the sleeping Bill Longee or Bar Fly. With breakfast finished they saddled and, obeying Felipe's commands, paired off.

Felipe and his partner, Carlos Garcia, took the country to the south and east of the ranch. There was, Felipe believed, no use in going on west. Whatever Bill had seen was between the Circle B and the Seven Slash. The other two Circle B riders were instructed to search the draws north and east of the ranch.

It was something after ten o'clock before Felipe made the discovery. Riding down an arroyo near the Seven Slash fence he saw the glint of an empty bottle. Rain and wind had long since washed away the wheel tracks of Bill Longee's cart, but Felipe rode toward the spot where the sun struck the glass. He recognized the type of bottle, a square high-shouldered extract bottle, but that meant nothing to him.

What did strike and hold his attention as he came closer was a small white object. Felipe called Carlos and got down from his horse. When Carlos arrived Felipe was down on his knees, scooping away sand. As he straightened up Carlos could see what Felipe had uncovered. Carlos crossed himself swiftly. There in the little depression that Felipe had made were the bones of a man's hand, stripped of flesh by vultures or coyotes. It lay there, mute evidence of what was underneath. Water, rushing down the arroyo, had stripped the sand partially away from the deep-buried body.

'Go to the house and bring a shovel,' Felipe commanded in Spanish. 'Pronto!'

Carlos nodded, climbed to his saddle and spurred up the draw.

CHAPTER FOURTEEN

Burt Randall

About the time that the Circle B crew was eating breakfast, Timmy Auliffe was having a horse saddled in her uncle Cal Summerford's livery barn. She promised her aunt that she would go to the Seven Slash and she intended to do so. She had made arrangements with Doctor Harper to have another take her place

194

with Bradford during the day, and she planned to spend her full time at the ranch. When the horse was saddled she rode back to Summerford's house, ate the breakfast that her aunt had prepared, and telling Cal and Maria that she would be back before dark, started out toward home.

As she rode south the girl pondered the things that she knew concerning Bradford's shooting. Scott McGuire had told her of the trail that Cody had found, and also told her that Cody had not followed it far. Timmy, despite Bradford's statement of the day previous, was still worried. Her father was in jail. She knew that Harper intended to talk to McGuire and she herself had told Cody of what Bradford had said. Still, Cody had not been too enthusiastic. He had cautioned her against letting her hopes rise too high. Timmy wondered if there were not something that she could do to aid Big Tim.

She was essentially active. She had gone to Harper's and undertaken Bradford's nursing simply because she could not let the man die and her father be branded a murderer. Now she had become genuinely fond of Bradford for his own sake. The man, weak, barely living, was so patient, so strong-willed, his eyes followed her with such dogged devotion, that she had come to like him a great deal. If Bradford lived and if Tim were cleared of the charge against him, Timmy was positive that she could bring them together. Too, her first hot anger against Cody Venture had died. The girl realized fully now the type of man Cody was, and realizing that, knew that Cody could not have acted differently.

As she thought of Cody her recollection went back to the night in the cavern under Cochise Head. From that the train of recollection followed to the next day when she had left Cody sleeping, ridden to the Seven Slash and seen her father. On that day she had gone to the fence and met Clay Stevens. She flushed angrily as she remembered Stevens' words. Stevens had said that if she were not too good to spend a night in the hills with Cody Venture, she was not too good for him. How had Clay Stevens known of the night in the cave? Little lines of concentration appeared between Timmy Auliffe's eyes. There was only one answer: Clay Stevens had been in the Chiricahuas himself that night.

And now Timmy Auliffe really began to think. Clay Stevens must have been somewhere close to the cave under Cochise Head. That was evident. Timmy knew of the payroll robbery, of course. She also knew that two of the bandits had escaped from the posse after the fight in Rustlers' Park. That was common talk. On the night that Bradford had been shot someone had left a trail from the Seven Slash fence up toward the rocks and the head of Bonita Canyon. A sudden resolve

196

formed in Timmy's mind. She would not go to the ranch. Instead she would ride up the fence, circle Bonita and then work over to the country under Cochise Head. There might be something there. She might learn something of importance, something that would help her father, and—Timmy admitted Cody to her thoughts—something that would help Cody too. So, instead of going on toward the Seven Slash, Timmy Auliffe turned Cry Baby to the left. There was no use in going to the ranch when she meant to strike into the hills.

Timmy had laid out a big day for herself, a day that would have worn out a man. She gave no thought to that. Cry Baby went along, following almost the same path that the posse had taken on the morning following the payroll robbery. Timmy struck into the hills on the west side of Rough Mountain and, in a familiar country, followed along toward the south.

It was ten o'clock when she reached the head of Bonita Canyon and came to the spires, pinnacles and misshapen gnomes that nature had cut from the ryolite. With Cry Baby picking his footing the girl worked along through the rocks. She had no very definite idea of what she was looking for or what she hoped to accomplish. She stopped her horse on a ridge and sat there, looking over the country from that point of command. Timmy saw nothing of particular interest, but she was seen. As she rode down from the ridge a man crawled back into a cave and spoke to another.

'Somebody up on the ridge, Bill.'

The man he addressed stirred and came forward to join the speaker. 'Gettin' close to us?' he questioned. 'I wonder if that damn' Clay . . .'

Timmy was coming down from the ridge, not realizing that she was following a trail. Cry Baby knew, however. Cry Baby knew that horses had been along ahead of him. Timmy rode easily, scanning the country. Cry Baby suddenly tossed his head and nickered. From Timmy's right a shrill neigh answered. Timmy stopped her horse. There ought not to be horses in this country. A horse meant a rider, perhaps the very rider she was looking for.

As she stopped Cry Baby, a man appeared at the edge of a rock. Timmy recognized him. Bill Lackey, who had ridden for the Circle B. 'What are you doing here, Bill?' demanded Timmy Auliffe.

Bill Lackey came forward. Behind him another man appeared, a man that Timmy did not know.

'I'm just up here,' said Bill vaguely. 'What are you doin' up here, Miss Auliffe?'

'I'm looking . . .' began Timmy, and stopped short. The man behind Bill had produced a gun. He held it squarely on Timmy.

'Get down!' ordered the man with the gun. 'Lookin', were you? Well, if you ask me, you looked too damn' much.'

Timmy got down. Bill Lackey was arguing with the other man, telling him that he was a fool. The other man kept his gun pointed, and answered the argument.

'Mebbe I'm a fool,' he said. 'Mebbe I ain't. Anyhow, she's goin' to stay right here 'til Clay comes in. She's been proddin' around too damn' free, if you ask me.'

Bill subsided. He took Cry Baby's reins and led the horse away. The man with the gun gestured toward the rock around which he had come. 'You go in there,' he directed. 'You ain't goin' to be hurt if you behave.'

Timmy went around the rock.

On the far side of the rock there was a crack in the rock wall, the entrance to a cave. Timmy entered under direction. It was dim inside the cave but she could see tumbled bedding, a part of a camp outfit. The man with the gun gestured toward the bedding.

'Set down,' he said. His voice was rough but not unkind. 'You can't get away afoot an' you can't get a horse. Don't try.'

Timmy sat down. Bill Lackey came in and looked at her. 'You hungry?' he questioned, and then without waiting for an answer, 'I'll get you a snack.'

He busied himself beside a blackened place where there had been a fire. Timmy looked at the other man. She felt a little weak inside. The other man had put away the gun. He was staring at her.

'What were you doin' up here?' he demanded.

'I . . .' Timmy hesitated, not sure what she should say. She couldn't tell the truth. She couldn't say that she was looking for payroll bandits, nor could she say that she had been searching for a man who had made a trail from the Seven Slash fence on the night of the Gantrys' dance.

'If you hadn't been so ringy she wouldn't be in here,' snapped Bill, looking up from his work.

The other man looked crestfallen.

'She'd of gone right on by,' amplified Bill.

The other man said, 'Hell! I'm goin' to keep her here 'til Clay comes up.'

'Clay Stevens?' asked Timmy.

'Clay Stevens,' answered the other man.

Bill Lackey brought over a big chunk of meat placed between cold halves of sourdough biscuits. 'Here,' he said, 'eat this.'

Timmy took the sandwich.

*　　　*　　　*

Cody Venture and Scott McGuire didn't get away from Bowie as they had planned. During the night there had been a fight in the native town across the tracks. A man had been cut with a knife and Scott had official duties to attend to. The knife-wielder had departed for

200

points unknown and the injured man, though not seriously hurt, had demanded the attention of the officers. It was noon before Scott was ready to go, and he decided that they might as well eat dinner before they began their trip.

While the two ate, the noon train came in and as they left the restaurant they saw Verne Richards approaching. Richards, the sheriff of Cochise county, was a small man, square and weathered and hard. He wore a grey goatee that jutted forward like the bow of a clipper ship. His eyes were blue, with sun wrinkles at the corners, and he perpetually chewed tobacco that leaked down on the grey goatee. Cody liked Richards. Every law-abiding citizen of Cochise county liked Richards.

The sheriff saw his deputy and the young marshal and approached them. He greeted the two, shook hands, and smiled faintly at Cody.

'Kind of had your hands full down here, ain't you, Venture?' he said. 'I had a talk with Pendergast an' he said you'd been busy.'

Cody nodded. 'Pretty busy,' he answered.

'You got your fence business 'tended to yet?' asked Richards.

Cody shook his head. 'They'll be down shortly,' he answered. 'I think we maybe got a lead on that Douglas payroll business, Mr. Richards. Some of that money turned up in Wilcox. Scott and I are going to look into it today.'

Richards spat a brown stream and wiped his mouth with the back of his hand. 'That's why I'm down here,' he said. 'I was in Wilcox yesterday. Some of that money was there.'

'That's where I got it,' Cody squinted his grey eyes and looked at the sheriff. 'You know who had it, Mr. Richards?'

'It narrowed down to a few,' answered Richards carefully. 'Who were you goin' to look up, Cody?'

'We were goin' up into the country above Bonita,' answered McGuire. 'You know, Verne, when we run into them fellows up there two of 'em got away into the rocks. Cody saw the trails. We worked out that country pretty careful a time or two, but we didn't find a thing.'

'An' you think you can now?'

Cody nodded.

'Hmmmmm,' said Richards. 'I think you can, too. You know there's been a filin' made on the head of Bonita?'

Both Cody and McGuire bobbed their heads.

'Well,' Richards spoke casually, 'I'd come over to see the fellow that made that filin'.'

'Stevens?'

'Stevens,' agreed Richards.

'Did he spend that payroll money?' McGuire lost his customary drawl.

'No,' Richards shook his head, 'but it seems like some of the men with him did. Either of

202

you boys know a fellow named Wig Parsons?'

'He used to work for the Circle B,' Cody said slowly. 'I think he's with Clay now; I saw him in Wilcox the day I left.'

Richards turned briskly. 'Well,' he announced, 'we might as well get at it. I want to go up to Stevens' place. You boys can come along.'

'We were goin' there,' replied McGuire. 'We . . . What in hell is this?'

The exclamation was caused by the appearance of a little crowd in the street. There were horsemen and a wagon, all surrounded by curious townspeople. Cody recognized one of the riders. It was Felipe de Cespedes.

The three officers hurried toward the crowd, broke through it and stopped beside the wagon. Felipe had seen them coming and had dismounted. He grinned flashingly at Cody, nodded to McGuire and Richards and greeted the three.

'I'm bring something in to you, Scott,' he said. 'We find something.'

'What have you got in the wagon?' snapped McGuire.

'Mebbe,' Felipe looked round, 'we better go some place where we don't have so many people.'

'The wagon yard,' said Cody.

Felipe nodded. Richards and McGuire faced the crowd.

'We won't need you fellers,' said McGuire pointedly.

Cody led the way to Summerford's wagon yard. The wagon, flanked by Felipe and his men and with Richards and McGuire walking beside it, followed. At the gate to the yard the crowd stopped. Felipe, the wagon and the men with it, went in. Cody swung the gate shut. Outside curious men applied their eyes to the openings between the gate palings. Well toward the middle of the yard the driver halted the wagon team and the mounted men swung down.

'Well?' said Richards, facing Felipe de Cespedes.

Felipe eyed the sheriff. 'Las' night,' he said, speaking slowly, 'Bill Longee an' Bar Fly come drunk to the ranch. Bill was scared an' Bar Fly was asleep. Bill talks much about Burt Randall. He says that Burt's head is shot open an' his brains leak. I think Bill is loco. He talks about arroyos an' he's getting fired an' play the fiddle an' it is all mixed up so I give him two more drinks an' he goes to sleep. Then I sit down an' I think that Bill maybe see something in an arroyo. So this morning me an' my men ride the arroyo east of the house and me an' Carlos find this.'

Felipe pulled back the tarp that covered the wagon bed. The men, Richards, McGuire, and Venture, looked at what was revealed. They stepped back quickly after that first look and even the weathered face of Richards was a little white.

'It's Burt, all right,' McGuire stated, his voice shaken.

Felipe was meticulously rolling a cigarette. He finished the process, lit it and puffed once. 'An' if he's got brains they leak out all right,' said Felipe. 'The back of his head is all gone.'

Richards stared at Cody and McGuire. 'What could have done that?' he asked.

'Who? . . .'

'I don't know,' said Cody. 'I can tell you this, though. Felipe an' me was at the Circle B. Stevens an' the whole crew had quit Bradford an' we helped him out a little. We found a piece of blanket in the fireplace at the bunkhouse an' it had Randall's initials on it.' He reached in his pocket, produced the charred cloth and held it out to Richards.

Richards took the piece of blanket in his hands and examined it. 'It looks like,' drawled Verne Richards, looking up at Cody, 'we'd mebbe have a little somethin' else to ask Stevens when we find him. Somethin' besides what Wig Parsons was doin' with those bills.'

They adjourned from the wagon yard, leaving the stolid Carlos on watch. There were things to do now, other things than to saddle horses and ride to the Chiricahuas. Scott McGuire set about summoning the Justice of the Peace and a coroner's jury. Verne Richards and Cody walked down the street. They had gone but a short distance when Doctor Harper joined them. Harper had been looking for Cody.

'Bradford's feeling pretty good today,' he said. 'He wants to talk to you, Venture.'

'And I want to talk with him,' agreed Cody. 'Can Mr. Richards go with me?'

Harper nodded. 'Bradford wants to clear up this thing about Auliffe,' he said. 'It will do him good to get it off his mind.'

'We can go right with you,' said Richards, eyeing the doctor. 'Scott won't be ready for a while an' this other thing can wait.'

Cody nodded, and turning, they accompanied the doctor.

On the way to the house Harper spoke encouragingly of Bradford's condition. 'It looks as though he'll pull through,' said the doctor. 'The wound was never very bad. It was the loss of blood that hurt. Timmy Auliffe has stayed right there and nursed him and that has helped a lot. Bradford has been fretting all day because she's gone.'

'Gone?' Cody echoed the word.

'She went out to the ranch,' said Harper. 'She needed to get out. She's been kept in mighty close.'

The three went into the doctor's home and Harper conducted them down the hall, cautioning them as he walked against exciting Bradford or asking too many questions. The doctor opened a door and motioned for Cody and Richards to go in.

Bradford lay on a bed near the window. His face was waxen, pallid, the lips colorless; his hands, lying on the coverlet, were white and thin, and the veins stood out in colorless ridges. Bradford moved his head as the men entered, and smiled faintly. Mrs. Harper rose from a chair and bustled out of the room.

'This is Mr. Richards, the sheriff, Mr. Bradford,' said Cody, nodding towards Richards. 'Doctor Harper said you wanted to see me so I brought Richards along.'

Bradford moved his eyes but said nothing. He was husbanding his strength. Cody spoke again. 'Doctor Harper said you wanted to make a statement about what happened,' he said. 'Would you like to have me write it down?'

Now Bradford spoke. 'Yes,' he said faintly. 'I'll sign it.'

Harper hurried out to return with pen, ink and paper. Cody moved a table close to the bed and seated himself. When Cody was ready Bradford began.

'I left Gantry's,' he said, pausing between the words. 'I had gone quite a distance when I decided to turn back and see if I could not talk with Mr. Auliffe again. I wanted to talk with him about our ranches.'

Cody's pen scratched busily as Bradford paused. 'You wanted to tell Tim Auliffe that there could be some sort of agreement made about a line between the places, didn't you, Mr. Bradford?' Cody asked.

Bradford said, 'Yes.'

Cody wrote again. 'I've written that in,' he announced.

Bradford's weak voice continued. 'Auliffe was intoxicated when I saw him earlier in the evening. He lost his temper but I hoped that we could get together.'

Again Cody wrote while the man on the bed paused.

'I'd ridden back perhaps a quarter of a mile,' Bradford spoke again. 'I heard a horse coming and I stopped and called to the rider. There was no answer but the horse came nearer.'

The pen scratched on the paper. 'Yes?' said Cody.

'The man came up.' Bradford seemed to gain a little strength. 'I could see the horse and the outline of the rider. I am positive that it was not Tim Auliffe. I asked who it was. He didn't answer but leaned forward on the horse and fired at me. I fell and struck the ground. I heard more movement and then I must have fainted.'

'And you're sure it wasn't Tim Auliffe?' Richards interjected the question.

'Sure,' agreed Bradford.

'Do you have any idea who it was?'

'No,' said the man on the bed.

Cody finished writing. 'I've said here that

you make this statement of your own free will,' he announced. 'Will you sign it now?'

'This will clear Mr. Auliffe, won't it?' asked Bradford.

'It'll help,' said Richards.

'I'll sign it.'

Cody dipped the pen again and brought the written sheet and the pen to the bed. Bradford's hand was limp. He managed to scrawl his name and Cody again took the paper and the pen.

'Doctor Harper and I will sign as witnesses,' he announced.

Harper signed his name and straightened up. 'In about three weeks you will be out of here helping round up the man who shot you,' he informed Bradford, cheerfully. 'All you need now is to get some strength. Your wound is healing fine.'

Bradford essayed a wan smile. 'Where is Miss Auliffe?' he asked.

'She's gone to the ranch,' said Harper. 'I told her she had to get out for a while and you are coming along so well she took a vacation.'

'She is a fine girl,' said Bradford, and closed his eyes.

Harper went to the door and called his wife. When she had come he escorted Cody and Richards out of the sickroom.

As they left the doctor's house Richards spoke to Cody. 'It don't look like there's any more need of holdin' Tim,' he said. 'There's some things that's got to be cleared up such as that gun in Tim's saddle pocket an' Tim's trail from where Bradford was shot, but I think that we can get the J.P. to set bail an' turn Tim loose. What do you think, Cody?'

Cody hesitated. 'I thought that maybe with Tim in jail, the fellow that really did this might get careless,' he answered. 'If you say so, though, I guess we could turn Tim out.'

'I do say so.' Richards was positive. 'Jails ain't good for old-timers like Tim. We'll see about it.'

When the two reached the main street they found Scott McGuire waiting for them. Scott had impaneled a coroner's jury and he had two telegrams for Cody. The messages were from the customs men at Douglas and Nogales, answering his inquiry concerning the D Cross cattle. There was no record of any such cattle being crossed at either place. Cody showed the wires to Richards and McGuire.

'It looks like there'd have to be a round-up of Circle B an' D Cross stuff,' he said. 'I think I'll wire to Nogales an' have the chief inspector come up here.'

Richards nodded and McGuire spoke. 'You seem mighty anxious about it,' grinned McGuire. 'I reckon you'd like to find all them D Crosses was smuggled cattle.'

'I would,' Cody said seriously. 'It would just about save Tim's bacon if the D Cross stuff was impounded for duty.'

210

'Go ahead an' wire the inspector,' said Richards. 'You say you're all ready, Scott?'

McGuire nodded and the three men walked on. As they reached the jail where the jury and the Justice of the Peace were waiting Cody showed McGuire Bradford's signed statement. McGuire nodded after he had read it and Richards told his deputy that he intended to have bail set for Tim Auliffe.

'I can fix it with the district attorney all right,' said Richards. 'He ain't been overly active in this case, anyhow.'

There was some friction between the sheriff's office and that of the district attorney. Cody and McGuire were silent.

It took time to conduct the inquest. The jury viewed the remains of Burt Randall, heard Felipe de Cespedes and Carlos Garcia, and listened while Cody told of finding the remnant of Randall's blanket in the Circle B bunkhouse.

Under instruction of the Justice, the jury brought in a verdict, finding that Burt Randall had come to his death at the hand of a person or persons unknown to them.

With the jury dismissed, Verne Richards still had business for the Justice of the Peace. He asked for and received a John Doe warrant for Randall's murderer and produced Bradford's statement with the suggestion that Tim Auliffe's hearing be reopened.

The J.P. was willing. He reopened the

hearing, admitted Bradford's statement as evidence, and heard Cody's statement concerning the other trail to the Seven Slash. When that was done the Justice set bail for Tim Auliffe.

Cal Summerford was sought and willingly signed Tim's bond, and Meyers, the storekeeper, agreed to be the other signer. The bond signed and posted, Scott McGuire released Tim Auliffe from his cell and brought him to the jail's little office.

Tim and Richards shook hands. Auliffe was silent. He could not comprehend his release and it took both Richards and Cody to acquaint the big owner of the Seven Slash with the facts. When Tim finally realized just what had happened he shook hands with Richards again and expressed a desire to see Bradford.

'I've come to know he's a good man,' said Tim Auliffe. 'I'd like to thank him.'

'You can't see him now,' said Cody. 'Doc Harper just let us in for a minute, long enough to get this statement. Mebbe in another week you can see him, Tim.'

Auliffe nodded his shaggy white head and considered Cody thoughtfully.

Richards took charge of the conversation. 'I think you'd better go out to the Seven Slash an' stay there, Tim,' he said. 'This ain't all cleared up an' you're just out on bail. I'm goin' to stay here a while an' see what I can do, an' Cody's got some ideas he wants to work on.'

'Where's Timmy?' asked Big Tim.

'She's at the ranch,' answered Cody. 'I think like Mr. Richards does, Tim. You'd better go out there.'

Auliffe nodded. 'I'll go out tonight,' he said decisively. 'Cody, I give Johnny Bowen orders about the fence. I told him to start takin' it down.'

'I heard,' said Cody. 'I don't think that Johnny's done much about it yet.'

'I will,' promised Auliffe. 'I'll start right out. I reckon I was wrong about you, Cody. I reckon . . .' Auliffe broke off. It was hard for him to confess his fault. He eyed Cody doubtfully.

Cody took a step and seized Tim Auliffe's hand. 'We'll say nothin' about it,' he said swiftly. 'You're all right, Tim.'

Tim Auliffe looked away, one hand brushing his eyes, and then turned back to the men in the office.

'I'm a damn' old fool,' he grated. 'One thing you boys won't have to worry about. I ain't drinkin' no more.'

'That's good, Tim.' Richards spoke cheerfully. 'Now I reckon we better clear out of here. You'll want to start to the ranch before it's any later an' I want to get organized. Let's go.'

They left the office. Scott McGuire parted from the group to arrange for the burial of Burt Randall's body, and Cody and Richards walked down to the livery barn with Tim Auliffe. There Tim got a horse and borrowed a saddle from Summerford. When the horse was saddled the big man climbed up slowly and looked down at the two men on the ground.

'I ain't goin' to forget this,' he said. 'I . . .' He leaned down, shook hands with Richards and with Cody, and then turned his horse and started out of town.

When Auliffe had left, Richards and Cody looked at each other. Richards grunted. 'Damn' good lesson,' he said. 'I . . . Hell, Cody! There's just a few old-timers left.'

Cody nodded. 'I'm goin' to send a wire to Nogales,' he announced. 'When do you want to pull out, Mr. Richards?'

Verne Richards looked at the sun, hovering over the Dos Cabezas. 'Early in the mornin',' he answered. 'Is there anybody you want to take along?'

'I'd like to take Felipe,' answered Cody. 'His brother Juan was killed, you know, an' it seems kind of like Felipe ought to go.'

'Get him,' said Richards. 'I'll see you at supper.'

CHAPTER FIFTEEN

The Posse Rides

It was evident to Cody Venture that Verne Richards, wise in the ways of the border country, contemplated a serious expedition. Richards organized a posse. He did very little talking about it and he didn't tell the men he chose just what his objective was, but he made careful selections. When the sheriff, his deputy, and Cody ate their supper together, Richards casually mentioned the men he had selected. There were, of course, Cody and Scott McGuire. In addition Cody had spoken to Felipe de Cespedes. Richards had sworn in Wyatt Brown and Cal Summerford, and said that he wanted another man.

'You must figger on a battle, Verne,' said McGuire.

Richards shook his head. 'I'm takin' men enough to fight a battle if I have one,' he said. 'What I want is men that know the country an' that I can depend on. I'm goin' to take 'em. The county's got a little money an' it might as well be spent on deputies.'

After the meal the men adjourned to Bud Jessop's Alcatraz Saloon. McGuire and Richards, with Jessop and Meyers, started a five-cent-ante poker game, and Cody, with

Felipe, watched the play. Felipe had sent his riders back to the Circle B with the wagon that had brought in Randall's body.

The game lasted late. No one seemed to want to go to bed in spite of the hard day that probably lay ahead. No one was winning or losing a great deal of money but both players and spectators were enjoying the session. About eleven o'clock Verne, dealing, declared that this was his last hand. He had dealt the cards and picked up his hand when a horse slid to a stop outside the Alcatraz and Johnny Bowen, disheveled and dust covered, came through the door. The men at the poker table came to their feet.

'Timmy ain't at the ranch,' snapped Johnny Bowen, wasting no words. 'She ain't been there all day. Tim sent me in to tell you.'

They all gathered around the Seven Slash rider. Bowen's story was short. He and the other two Seven Slash riders had been working at the fence all day, removing wire and posts. They had come in to the supper that Bill Longee had prepared, Bill and his crony Bar Fly having returned to the Seven Slash sometime while the men were out. After supper there had been a pitch game in the bunkhouse which Tim Auliffe's arrival had interrupted.

Tim had asked at once for Timmy and a hasty search about the place had disclosed that the girl had not been there. Immediately Tim had sent Bowen to town with the news and he and the other two men were out with lanterns, searching the country north of the Seven Slash hoping to find some trace of the girl.

Bowen scarcely finished talking before general activity struck the Alcatraz. Cody went to the livery stable and found that Timmy had left early that morning, bound for the Seven Slash. She had been riding Cry Baby and the hostler had seen her leave town.

A brief interview with Cal and Maria Summerford disclosed the fact that the girl had not returned from the Seven Slash and that they had not seen her since breakfast. Cal had supposed that with Tim at home, Timmy had decided to stay at the ranch and so neither he nor his wife had been unduly alarmed.

Cody wanted to leave immediately in search of the girl but Richards restrained him.

'No use of startin' until it's light,' snapped Richards. 'We can't do a thing in the dark. You know the horse she rode?'

Cody replied that he did.

'Know the horse well enough to trail it?' Richards was insistent.

'I think so,' answered Cody. 'Cry Baby has a narrow heel on the nigh front foot and he toes in a little. I've shod him for Timmy.'

Richards nodded. 'She started for the Seven Slash,' he said decisively. 'Tim's comin' in along the road. We'll ride out to meet him. If she's been throwed the horse will come in to the ranch. If she's still with the horse she may have thought of goin' some place else. Who would she visit out that way?'

'There's Lance Blount,' said Cody doubtfully. 'She might go to his place but if she went there she'd turn more east an' go around the mountains.'

'Tim will find her if she's along the road,' said Richards reassuringly. 'If he don't find her we'll go out in the mornin' an' pick up her tracks. Now if you want to ride out an' meet Tim, let's go.'

Cody led the way out of the Alcatraz. The men saddled horses in the livery barn, Cal Summerford joining them there. Wyatt Brown was aroused and he, too, joined them. With horses saddled, they secured additional lanterns from Meyers' store and, lighting them, started out of town, taking the road that ran south.

They spread out on both sides of the road, forming a long line. Cody, because he was familiar with Cry Baby's tracks, held the road. Next to Cody was Brown, and on the other side was Felipe. Beyond Felipe and Brown were Scott McGuire and Summerford, and beyond those two were Johnny Bowen and Richards. So, like an uneven line of fireflies, they rode south.

They did not find Timmy Auliffe. In a place or two Cody was able to identify Cry Baby's tracks, getting down from Walking John and

218

examining the earth to do so. At these spots he called the others to him so that they too might familiarize themselves with the distinctive prints Timmy's horse had left. They rode slowly, examining the road and the country about it, now and then checking restive horses and listening, hoping to hear a call. They heard nothing, found nothing.

When the little party of horsemen had traversed eight of the twenty miles that lay between Bowie and the Seven Slash boundaries, they saw lights approaching. Tim Auliffe and his two men were coming. They went ahead, met Auliffe and his riders, and stopped.

Tim Auliffe was half crazed. The big man, his eyes red and his face strained, could scarcely talk. Again it was Richards who took command.

'She's turned off the road some place,' Richards said grimly. 'As soon as it's light we'll find the place. Right now the thing for us to do is to head back to town in a bunch. We don't want to cover any tracks she's left. Maybe we've done that already. Let's go.'

As a group they obeyed the sheriff. Riding wide of the road they returned to Bowie.

Morning was streaking the sky grey when they reached the town. They left their lanterns at the livery stable, consulted with Bud Jessop who was waiting for them as to sending out other search parties later in the day, and again started out over the ground they had covered. Now Big Tim Auliffe and Cody Venture rode side by side, just out of the ruts that were the road, watching the ground, trying, searching with anxious eyes, to discern signs that they could recognize.

It was Cody who first saw Cry Baby's tracks and definitely identified them. He called the others in and they consulted, then rode on. Again Big Tim found the trail and knew that Timmy had come that way, but it was Felipe de Cespedes, far to the left of the others, who came upon a patch of smooth sand, stopped and raised a shout.

The party congregated swiftly. Felipe pointed to what he had found and Cody and Big Tim, dismounting, searched the place. They found in the firm sand a track of a horse with a narrow heel. Further along were other tracks. There was a mark where a front foot pointed in. They went on and in another open spot found more sign. Tim faced Cody and questioned him with his eyes. Cody nodded.

'It was Cry Baby,' he said definitely. 'He come this way.'

Felipe, adept at tracking, added his word. 'She was ridin',' said Felipe. 'The horse stays in line an' does not wander.'

Verne Richards raised his eyes toward the hills, now beginning to be tipped with the sun. 'We'll work it out careful, boys,' said Verne Richards. 'It looks like she headed to the

Chiricahuas.'

'Likely she went to the Blounts.' Cody afforded Big Tim what consolation he could. 'She changed her mind and decided to go to Lance's place.'

Big Tim nodded but there was a worried look in his eyes.

'Why don't you go to Blount's, Tim?' questioned Richards. 'You'll find her there.'

Big Tim shook his head. 'I'll stay with you,' he said slowly. 'If we strike her tracks in a trail that goes to Blount's I'll ride ahead.'

Richards nodded and again they took up progress.

With so many men in the party, they traveled rapidly. When the trail broke they separated, circled, some dismounting, and presently would find the tracks again. These men were expert. When a shod hoof had slipped on a rock, where Timmy had twisted aside to avoid catsclaw or mesquite, where Cry Baby had torn out a mouthful of coarse grass in passing, they saw the sign. Only solid rock would baffle them. They swung under Rough Mountain and Cody, McGuire and Richards, drawing together, looked at each other.

'She ain't headed for Blount's,' said McGuire, low-voiced, giving expression to the thought uppermost in the minds of the other two.

'Can't you go through this way?' questioned Richards.

'You can but it isn't a good trail,' answered Cody.

'Mebbe . . .' Scott McGuire began.

'Mebbe she got an idea like we had,' said Richards. 'We might attend to our business on this trip anyhow. If we find her up here we can send her back with Tim an' go on.'

Cody and McGuire nodded and once more they swung apart.

Beyond the Rough Mountain country the trail was more difficult to follow. Timmy had meandered from one high point to another, searching the country, and the men that followed her wasted time. Finally they came to the maze of rocks above Bonita Canyon, definitely lost the trail, and stopped. By that time it was noon. The sun was straight overhead. The possemen dismounted and gathered about Richards. Consultation followed, each speaker being careful of what he said, fearing to alarm Tim Auliffe.

'She went through the rocks,' said Richards, speaking absently. 'She sure come in here.'

'Timmy always liked it up here,' said Cody, looking at Big Tim. 'She might of decided to come up here just for the ride.'

'But where did she go from here?' Big Tim blurted the words. 'She didn't go to the ranch. She wouldn't have gone to Blount's from here. Where is she?'

Respecting the terror in Tim's eyes, the others turned their heads away.

It was Cody who spoke again. 'Clay Stevens told me in Wilcox,' said Cody steadily, 'that he'd homesteaded above Bonita. There's a little park down below the rocks. That's likely where he'd build his cabin. We'd better go down there and if we find anybody ask them if they've seen Timmy. Mebbe her horse fell with her an' she's afoot.'

Richards took the suggestion. 'We'll do that,' he said. 'Lead out, Venture. You know the way.'

They mounted again and with Cody in the lead left the rocks and started west. Within half an hour they came to the little mountain park.

There were buildings in the park, or rather the beginnings of buildings. Logs had been cut and laid for foundations, and as the Bowie men rode in a man came from behind one of these sites and advanced toward them. Cody recognized the man as a former Circle B rider, Bill Lackey.

The horsemen stopped and Lackey came up, a question written on his face. Richards made known their errand.

'You seen Timmy Auliffe?' he asked. 'She started out from Bowie yesterday mornin' headed for the ranch. She didn't get there. We followed her trail up to the rocks an' then lost it. Seen her?'

Lackey shook his head. Cody was watching the man intently. There was something in

Lackey's eyes that Cody didn't like.

'I ain't saw her,' said Lackey. 'She ain't been through here.'

'Is this Clay Stevens' place?' asked Cody, glancing about the park.

Lackey nodded. 'I reckon,' he said shortly.

'Clay here?' Richards took up the questioning.

'Naw.'

Cody looked at Richards. 'We might as well go on,' he said slowly. 'There's nothin' here. If you see the girl, shoot a couple of times, will you, Lackey?'

Lackey nodded. 'You comin' back?' he asked. Was there a tinge of anxiety in his voice?

'Not unless we hear you shoot,' answered Cody, before Richards could speak. 'We're goin' to work on down to the Seven Slash fence an' then back north. Then,' he spoke more slowly, 'we'll come back an' comb the rocks if we have to move 'em one at a time.'

Both Richards and McGuire seemed about to speak. Cody caught Richards' eyes. His own carried a warning. Richards refrained from voicing his thoughts.

'But . . .' McGuire interposed.

'Come on!' Cody's order was rough. 'Come on, Tim!'

He moved his horse. Walking John started across the little park. Perforce the others followed. The trees at the far side of the park

224

closed around them. Silently Cody moved his hand, beckoning. Richards and McGuire spurred close. The others, following, watched the movement.

'He knew something,' snapped Cody as Richards reached his side. 'I watched his eyes. I'm goin' back an' watch him. You go on a piece an' then circle back.'

Richards nodded. 'I thought he was shifty,' he said. 'Go on, Cody.'

Cody swung Walking John. The others continued. Their horses clattered over a little rock slide. Cody dropped from Walking John, tied his neckerchief over the horse's nose, and leading him, started back. Where the trees began to thin he stopped, tied the horse, and then slipped back afoot toward the clearing.

For a time, from a vantage point behind a big pine, he watched the little opening. He saw nothing. Then suddenly Bill Lackey appeared, leading a horse. The man looked about the park, mounted, and started up the hill. Before he was out of sight Cody went back to Walking John. He reached the horse and mounted. For a moment he thought of spurring after the others and recalling them. Then he decided against that move. They would return shortly in any case. Cody pulled his book of cigarette papers from his pocket. He would leave a plain trail, plain enough for anyone. He didn't want to lose sight of Lackey. Tearing off a paper he impaled it on the spiky branch of a little tree and then rode on toward the park.

He did not cross the open park. Instead he circled it, now and again removing a paper from the book and putting it in a conspicuous spot. On the far side of the park he turned toward the rocks. He took pains now. Lackey might not be a fool. He might be watching his back trail. Cody picked a high spot, dismounted and went toward it. He climbed up the rock and searched the surroundings with his eyes. He was rewarded. He saw Lackey's horse rounding a pinnacle that sprang up from the barren ryolite. Cody piled rocks in a little mound, put a cigarette paper under the top stone, where it fluttered white in the little wind, and regaining Walking John, rode toward the spot where Lackey had disappeared.

Again, cautiously, he dismounted and stole around the rock. Again he saw the rider he followed. Again he piled rocks conspicuously and went on.

Now he progressed afoot. He left Walking John tied to a little knob of stone that was a natural and convenient hitching post. Ahead he could hear a horse scrambling over rocks. He must be close to Lackey's destination.

It seemed to Cody that the horse was making a great deal of noise. He stopped and looked around. There, just ahead, the wind and water had carved a gargoyle from the stone. Cody raised himself a little and peered over the edge. Two hundred yards away he could see two men, Bill Lackey and another. Lackey had dismounted from his horse. The two were arguing, as was evident from their gestures. Cody watched them. As he watched he saw another figure emerge from a crevice in the rock wall before which the men stood. A woman. Timmy Auliffe. The man with whom Bill Lackey argued turned to the girl, put his hand on her shoulder and shoved her toward the crevice. Timmy reeled under the force of that shove but caught herself before she fell.

Behind Cody Walking John nickered. He had rubbed off the neckerchief that bound his nose. That whistle was answered twice! The horse that Lackey rode lifted his head and neighed, and from somewhere to Cody's left and the rear, not one, but two, horses bugled.

Lackey whirled around. His companion seized Timmy and half carried her into the crevice in the rock wall. For an instant Lackey stood and then he, too, dived for the crevice, and from behind Cody Venture came a shot, another, and then a fusillade. The posse, following his trail, had encountered something!

CHAPTER SIXTEEN

Flight in the Rocks

After that first flat spatter of shots there was a moment's quiet. Cody could see the two men in the rock crevice. They were partially shielded by the rock which jutted to their left and they were too far for Cody to fire. He had a Colt under his arm, but his rifle was back on the saddle. Two hundred yards is not a good range for pistol practice. For Cody to call out or raise himself would be folly. He would expose his position without accomplishing anything. He lay flat, only his head lifted.

A voice was raised in a shout. Richards' voice. The sheriff called strongly: 'Stevens! This is Richards talkin'. I got a warrant for you.'

There was no answer. Richards called again. 'There's plenty here to take you, Stevens.'

There was an answer to that, a shot that spanked against the quiet of the air, struck a rock and whined away. Horses clattered on the rocks and Cody heard a man cursing somewhere nearby. He squirmed around to see who it was but the man was hidden by intervening rocks.

This was a madhouse. In that labyrinth of stone the men of the posse and the men they

228

were seeking would play hide and seek. Cody took a chance.

'Richards!' he called. 'Richards!'

The sheriff had shifted his position. He answered Cody's call. 'Yeah! That you, Cody?'

'It's me,' answered Cody. 'I got two of 'em spotted over against the ridge. They got Timmy!'

From Cody's immediate right came a bull-like bellow that could belong only to one person: Tim Auliffe. Immediately Cody was sorry he had called.

'Stay down, Tim,' he warned. 'Stay hid. We'll get her.'

Big Tim was cursing, working over the rocks, making toward the rock on which Cody lay. Others had identified that rock, as well as had Big Tim Auliffe. One of the men at the crevice had produced a rifle. A slug whined away from the rock at Cody's right. The top of that gargoyle was no place to be.

'Stay inside, Timmy,' yelled Cody, squirming backward on the rock. 'Stay out of it, girl!'

His boot toes protruded over the edge of the rock and he pulled himself further back. Below him a voice said sternly: 'Stay right there, jasper. I got you covered!'

'For cripe's sake, Wyatt!' expostulated Cody Venture.

Wyatt Brown chuckled. 'Come down off your perch,' he commanded. 'Come down quick, if it's you.'

Cody was going to take no chance of falling from that rock. The rifleman at the crevice had found the range and was making fair practice. Dust puffed up from the top of the rock. Cody rolled on his back, sat up hastily, and seeing where he would land, slid over the edge. The tail of his coat caught and tore but it broke his fall somewhat. He struck the rock below and Wyatt Brown seized him, holding him erect.

'We followed your trail, Cody,' said Brown. 'You plumb out of cigarette papers?'

Cody swore angrily and jerked himself away. 'Are you a plumb damn' fool?' he demanded. 'What happened, Wyatt?'

'We followed the trail you left,' replied Brown, with relish. 'Got right up to your pile of rocks an' seen Clay Stevens an' Wig Parsons an' two more comin' in from the west. About that time a horse whistled an' Tim's horse an' Scott's both answered. Stevens seen us an' Wig pulled a rifle out of his boot an' took a shot at Richards. Right then the fireworks started. How you makin' it?'

'There's a cave up against the lowest ledge,' announced Cody. 'That Lackey an' another fellow got Timmy in there. I saw her.'

'Hell!' spat Wyatt Brown. 'We're just playin' tag around amongst these rocks. Somebody's goin' to shoot a man he don't want to if we ain't careful.'

Apparently Richards had the same idea. He was calling from the rear, demanding that his men come to him.

'I reckon we'd better go,' said Brown, ruefully. 'What's your idea on this madhouse, Cody?'

Before Cody could reply there were three sharp reports within fifty yards, a pause and then two more shots. Felipe de Cespedes lifted his voice in a yelp of triumph.

'Felipe's got one of 'em,' rasped Brown. 'Come on, Cody.'

The two were forced to make a run between the rock that sheltered them, and the next. When they had gained it they paused for breath. Brown called, 'Felipe!' and was answered from a clump of rocks beyond.

Again they scurried across a gap, the riflemen at the ledge adding to their speed. When they gained shelter Brown called again and Felipe de Cespedes worked through a crevice and came to them.

'Who'd you get, Felipe?' demanded Brown. 'We heard you yip an' . . . Hell! You're hurt!'

Blood was dripping from Felipe's fingers, running down the blue left arm of his shirt.

'Es nada,' said Felipe. 'Me? I shoot somebody I don' know.'

Brown was stripping off his neckerchief 'Le's look at that arm,' he commanded. 'Then we'll go see the fellow you shot. Kill him?'

'He acts like dead,' corroborated Felipe, smiling flashingly.

Brown bared Felipe's arm. As he had said,

the wound was slight, a clean hole through the biceps. Brown bound it. They could still hear Richards calling.

'Bellers like a bull,' said Brown, tying the last knot. 'There. I guess that'll hold you. Where is this jasper?'

Felipe led the way back through the crevice and presently the three were standing looking down at a man. Cody shook his head.

'I don't know him,' he announced. 'How'd you get him, Felipe?'

Felipe grinned. 'I'm back around this rock,' he replied. 'I watch the ledge. We bump together. He's come the other way. We turn aroun' an' we don't ask questions, jus' shoot.'

'Well,' said Brown, 'you done a damn' good job, if you ask me. We'd better get back to Richards.'

Indeed the sheriff's voice was impatient and more than tinged with anger.

'Somebody will slip up on him an' put his light out,' said Brown, referring to the sheriff. 'We'd better hurry.'

Cody grunted. 'Verne Richards?' he said. 'Not him! He's in the middle of a clear place lookin' six ways at once an' a gun in each hand. Come on. We'll work back.'

They did work back. Clear of the clump of rock which had hidden them they found the going easier. Each man alert, with three to watch in varying directions, there was but little chance of surprise.

They found Richards, as Cody had suggested, in a little natural amphitheater. Johnny Bowen, Cal Summerford, and the two Seven Slash cowboys, Curly Archer and Rance Davis, had joined the sheriff. As Cody, Felipe and Brown came up, Scott McGuire appeared, leaving only Tim Auliffe unaccounted for.

'Where's Tim?' demanded Richards. 'He ain't been hurt, has he? Any of you see him?'

One after another the men shook their heads. 'I heard him yell,' said Cody. 'I called to you that there was two in a cave an' that they had Timmy. I heard Tim yell then.'

'You likely got him killed,' said Richards, sternly. 'Where is this cave?'

'It's in a ledge under the first bench,' answered Cody. 'We're on the second bench now.'

Richards grunted. 'We been playin' around like we were blindfold,' he said. 'There was three with Stevens. Wig Parsons an' two more. With two in the cave, that's six. There's nine of us. Nine against six . . .'

'Five,' said Wyatt Brown. 'Felipe stopped one, back a piece.'

'Five then,' said Richards. 'We can't count on Tim much but we got to look out for him. We . . .'

'We got to look out for Timmy, too.' Cody made the interruption.

'Don't I know it?' snarled Richards.

Cody's grey eyes were cold. 'I don't want to

butt in on you, Richards,' he said, 'but we're wastin' time here. Those fellows will get to the cave, an' they got Timmy. I don't want to stand here talkin'.'

'What do you want to do?' Richards scowled at the deputy marshal.

'I want about three of you boys to get high,' directed Cody. 'Watch the cave with rifles an' don't let anybody in or out. Then I want to be let alone. One man in these rocks can do a lot more than a bunch. He won't have to be watchin' for friends all the time.'

'Two men,' said Felipe quietly. 'I go with you, Cody.'

'We'll all go,' snapped Brown. 'You . . .'

Richards made instant decision. 'Cody's right,' he said. 'We'll hunt the high spots. Go ahead, Cody, an' watch out for Tim. He's apt to shoot before he looks close.'

Cody nodded. He knew that Tim Auliffe, loose and half mad, was an extra hazard.

'Come on,' he said. 'We'll work in toward the ledge an' then you boys take to the rocks. Watch that cave.'

There were nods of agreement. Cody turned and started back the way he had come, Felipe, soft footed for all his boots, striding beside him. As they moved, fresh firing broke out among the rocks ahead. Tim Auliffe was conducting a battle all his own.

Cody broke from a walk into a run, followed by the other men of the posse. Felipe stayed

234

close to Cody's elbow, his left arm, wrapped in Brown's big neckerchief, dangling beside him.

Out of the little opening they separated, only Felipe and Cody staying together. The firing had died down. Whether that meant that Big Tim Auliffe had been killed or that he had driven back the others, they could not know. Cody dared not call out. To do so would expose his position. Somewhere in the rocks ahead were Clay Stevens and three desperate men.

From the tail of his eye Cody saw Wyatt Brown taking to a tall rock. Brown pushed his rifle up and climbed like a squirrel. He gained the top, flattened out, and Cody saw him pull his gun to his shoulder. He was past the rock before Brown fired.

From the left a rifle spoke imperiously three times. Only a man like Verne Richards could shoot that fast. It must be the sheriff Cody had slowed down.

He heard Richards' voice, cool, calm, calling, giving information. 'I hit one man at the cave. Watch yourself, Cody. There's somebody to your right.'

Cody stopped short. To his left Felipe crouched against a small misshapen boulder. A dwarf cedar, clinging to a miserly niche in a clump of rocks, trembled. Cody watched it, his gun half raised.

Richards called again. 'Tim! Tim! Stay right where you are, Tim; don't move around.

Cody's in the rocks.'

Cody watched that cedar. So Tim Auliffe was alive. Well-being flooded Cody. Again the cedar trembled and Felipe threw three swift shots at it. The cedar bent under suddenly added weight. A man's torso took the place of the top of the tree, slipping down over it, and Cody, leaping aside, felt a tug at his coat sleeve.

From behind the rocks that held the cedar a man stepped deliberately into the open. Wig Parsons. Wig's hat was gone, his face was grimy, with a bloodstain down one cheek. The gun in his hand came up and belched, even as Cody fired.

Parsons took a mincing step and sat down, his gun clattering on the rocks. Cody looked at the man. How oddly Wig sat. As Cody stared, Wig tumbled forward.

From behind Cody, Richards called: 'Come out with your hands up then, an' bring the girl. Let her get clear of you.' Evidently the men in the cave had quit.

Cody stepped toward Wig Parsons. He heard Wyatt Brown's rifle chattering like a thing gone mad. The rifle ceased and Brown's lurid curses took the place of its racket.

'Damn him,' Wyatt Brown almost wept. 'He's got away! He's got a horse!'

Cody paused beside Wig Parsons. Behind him, in the maze of rocks, he could hear Richards shouting for the horses. Men were calling from their places of concealment. Cody added his voice to the others.

'It's done, Richards!' he called.

Richards did not answer. He was still shouting directions, ordering men to bring the horses. Clay Stevens was escaping, riding off from the fight unscathed and vicious and the posse was afoot.

Wyatt Brown continued to swear. He slid down from his rock and joined Cody. Rock slivers had struck Brown's cheek when a bullet had ricocheted from stone and the cheek was bleeding.

'Stevens, damn him,' swore Brown. 'He had a horse an' I couldn't stop him.'

Cody said nothing. The exhilaration of the fight was still upon him but with Brown's words he felt a sudden let down. With Stevens loose it was still all to do over. Richards came up, disgust written on his face, discouragement in every line of his body: He spat deliberately, leaving a brown stain on stone.

'The next time I leave a man with the horses I'm goin' to hobble him,' said Richards, eyeing the stone. 'The fool kid couldn't stay out of a fight. He had to go prospectin' with his rifle. Now we're afoot an' Stevens is ridin' off!'

Wyatt Brown grunted and Richards lifted his eyes and looked at the man. 'You might help find them horses, Wyatt,' he said. Brown grunted again, shifted his grip on his rifle and turned away, walking in the direction from which Richards had come. Cody bent down. He took Wig Parsons by the shoulders. Felipe picked up Parsons' feet. With Wig's limp body sagging between them they carried the wounded man to the ledge.

Big Tim was holding Timmy in his arms, comforting the girl. Bill Lackey stood by sullenly, his arms held shoulder-high, a Seven Slash cowboy and Johnny Bowen watching him. Richards came up and back in the rocks Cody could hear Wyatt Brown swearing at the other Seven Slash puncher, the boy who had left the horses to join the fight. Cody looked down at Wig Parsons.

The men of Richards' posse assembled. Wig Parsons was alive. Bill Lackey was alive and unhurt. Bill Lackey's partner was brought from the cave. He was very, very dead. Felipe accompanied the Seven Slash men to the place where he had met Cody. They came back carrying a body and then went back and brought another. Of the men in Stevens' crew all were accounted for save Stevens. The bodies were laid in the shade of the ledge and Richards bent over Wig Parsons and questioned him.

Parsons was dying. Hard-hit, he hung to life with a grim tenacity and he swore feebly when Richards told him that Clay Stevens had taken a horse and got away. Stevens, Wig Parsons said, was a dirty yellow thing too low to be called a dog.

'He's gone, Wig,' said Richards quietly. 'You're dyin'. You ain't got an hour. Did Stevens kill Burt Randall?'

Cody bent down and wiped foam-flecked blood from Parsons' lips. Parsons' protuberant eyes stared up at him.

'I like to got you, Venture,' said Parsons.

'Pretty near, Wig,' agreed Cody, quietly.

'If Clay had stuck . . .' said Wig.

'Did Stevens kill Randall?' Richards was insistent.

'He killed Burt,' Parsons said slowly. 'Killed him when they pulled that payroll job. Burt was gettin' too big for his pants. He wanted to cut a full share. Now Clay's killed me, damn him!'

'You're dyin', Wig,' reminded Richards.

'An' damn' near time, too,' answered Wig Parsons. 'I ought to been killed ten years ago.'

'What about Bradford?' demanded Cody. 'Did you an' Stevens have anything to do with that?'

The man on the ground gave a ghastly laugh. 'We had everythin' to do with it,' he said. 'Clay met Bradford comin' back from Gantry's. We'd been hangin' around there watchin'. I wanted to go to the dance but Clay was scared, the yellow-belly. We seen Bradford ride off an' we started to foller him. When he turned back we didn't stop quick enough. He yelled an' Clay cut him down. We was standin' there, tryin' to think what to do when Tim

Auliffe come up on his horse, drunk as a lord. He was so damn' drunk he couldn't talk an' didn't know nothin'. We tied him on his horse an' sent the horse along. I rode out a piece where I could watch him an' I opened the gate into the Seven Slash to let the horse through. Clay had put his gun in Auliffe's saddle bag when we found the old fool didn't have one. I took the rope off him when he got to the gate. We thought that would pin it on him.'

The man paused. 'It would have, too,' he said defiantly. 'I'd never of told if Clay hadn't run out on me.'

'And the payroll robbery,' insisted Richards. 'What about that, Wig?'

Parsons was weakening rapidly. 'Give me a drink,' he rasped. 'Give me a drink.'

Someone brought a bottle from the cave and Richards held it to Parsons' lips. The man swallowed, choked, swallowed again, and cursed when the bottle was taken from him.

'What about the payroll?' questioned Richards again.

'Clay an' Burt pulled that.' Parsons got his breath in a gasp. 'Them an' Bill Lomax an' a feller from New Mexico we called Dutch. You fellers killed Lomax an' Dutch. Clay an' Burt got away an' hit for this place. They cached the money an' then started for the ranch. Clay got behind Burt an' killed him in a draw. We burnt his blankets. I was goin' to take Burt's place, Clay said.'

Cody nodded. He knew now the meaning of the trails he had followed on that day, seemingly so long ago. Randall and Stevens had split before they hit the rocks and then come together again.

'How'd you find us, Richards?' rasped Parsons. 'How . . . ?'

'You spent some of that payroll money in Wilcox, Wig,' said Richards. 'We found it.'

'Stevens was goin' to start a ranch,' Parsons' voice was perceptibly weaker. 'I told him we couldn't use that money yet. I told him . . .'

'What about the D Cross cattle?' Cody bent down over the man. 'Where . . . ?'

But Wig Parsons was not listening. The man's yellowed eyeballs showed. A trickle of blood welled from the corner of his mouth. He coughed rackingly and the blood stream grew.

'The cattle, Wig.' Cody was kneeling beside the man now. 'The D Cross.'

'God damn Clay Stevens' heart!' gasped Wig Parsons. 'God . . .'

Cody arose from his knees. He looked at Verne Richards. Richards lifted his eyes from Parsons' face.

'There's still Stevens,' said Cody Venture.

They laid Wig beside the others. Big Tim Auliffe had quieted his daughter. While Richards, Cody, and Scott McGuire listened to her story the others searched the cave. They found money, a good deal of it, the remainder of the Douglas payroll. They finished their

241

search and gathered around Timmy.

Timmy told of starting for the ranch. She told of how, riding out from Bowie, she had decided to come to the rocks. 'I met Clay Stevens at the fence that day,' she said, looking at Cody from below long, tear-wet eyelashes. 'I'd heard a shot and I went over to see what it was.'

Cody nodded. He knew now what that shot had been. It had been the shot with which Clay Stevens had killed Burt Randall. Timmy wet her lips, ready to continue. There was an interruption. Hoofs sounded on the rocks. Wyatt Brown and the Seven Slash puncher appeared. They were mounted and each led horses.

'Found 'em clear below the rim,' said Wyatt Brown. 'They was hoggin' grass.' He eyed the Seven Slash puncher. The Seven Slash man hung his head.

Richards was scowling. 'We killed plenty of time here,' snapped Richards, his eyes on the Seven Slash rider. 'Killed time because you couldn't do what you was told. Stevens got away. You . . .'

'Easy,' said Cody, checking Richards. 'Go ahead, Timmy.'

Timmy Auliffe continued: 'Stevens said something that made me think he might have been up here,' she said slowly. 'I knew he hated father, and I knew he hated you, Cody, and Mr. Bradford. I thought that I might run

242

onto something that would help. I got up here in the rocks and a man stepped out and covered me with a gun. They kept me here. They weren't bad to me, they just kept me. They said that they were waiting for Stevens.' She stopped her recital. Cody turned from the girl and looked at Richards.

'Well?' he said.

Richards straightened decisively. 'We got to move,' he said. 'Thanks to bein' afoot Stevens is loose. Scott, you go to Bowie. You wire from there. I want this country bottled up tight. I don't want Stevens out of it. You wire Rodeo an' get word to Paradise an' Portal. Wire Douglas an' Wilcox. Bottle it up. Tim, I reckon you'll want to take Timmy to the ranch. You go ahead.' He looked at the Seven Slash puncher. 'Somebody's got to take these fellows in,' he concluded. 'I reckon yo're elected.'

Activity fell upon the posse. Cody went to Timmy and her father. 'I want to talk to Timmy a minute,' he said to Big Tim, and drew the girl aside. Timmy looked up at him.

'I got to know somethin', Timmy,' said Cody. 'What did Clay say to you at the fence? I've got to know.'

The girl's eyes were wide. 'He said that if I'd be good to him we could make things right for Big Tim,' she answered, low-voiced. 'He knew we'd been in the cave, and . . .'

'How did he know?'

'He must have seen us, Cody. He . . .'

'That's what I wanted,' said Cody, tightly. 'Thanks, Timmy.'

'Cody, you're not going to . . .' Timmy clung to Cody's arm. Cody laid a reassuring hand on the girl's shoulder.

'You go to the ranch with Tim,' he said comfortingly. 'I'll be down to see you, Timmy. Just as soon as I can. I'm never goin' to be very far away from you again.'

He let the girl go and Big Tim, seeing Cody step away, came to his daughter. He took the girl's arm and Timmy walked away with him. The men were bringing the horses from where they had been left. Bill Lackey, hands down now, directed Johnny Bowen to where the outlaws' horses had been kept. Felipe de Cespedes came to Cody's side.

'I'm still remember Juan, Cody,' said Felipe.

'You better go in an' get that arm 'tended to,' said Cody.

Felipe shook his head. 'You an' me got one thing more to do,' he answered.

Cody shrugged. 'All right,' he said absently. 'All right, Felipe.'

The possemen loaded bodies on horses, lashing them across the saddles. Scott McGuire had already departed. Richards, directing operations, turned as Cody came to him.

'I reckon,' said Cody easily, 'that we won't go in with you, Richards. Felipe an' me are goin' to stay in the hills.'

'There'll be several stay,' snapped Richards. 'There's grub in that cave an' we can start from here in the mornin'. Scott's goin' to organize things outside.'

Cody nodded. 'If it's all right with you, Felipe an' I will pull out pretty quick,' he said. 'We can eat a bite an' go.'

'He'd better have a doctor look at that arm.' Richards was doubtful. 'I'd figured to send him out with the horses.'

Cody's lips tightened into a smile. 'You don't know Felipe,' he said.

'Suit yourself.' Richards shrugged. 'You can't go far before it's dark, though.'

'No,' agreed Cody, 'we can't.'

CHAPTER SEVENTEEN

Clay Stevens

The possemen finished loading the horses and with Bowen and a Seven Slash man in charge, the funeral train left. Timmy and Big Tim had already departed. The men wished to spare Timmy as much as they could and had sent the old ranchman and his daughter on ahead. With Bowen and the Seven Slash puncher went Bill Lackey, thoroughly tied and fastened to his horse. Wyatt Brown, Richards, Rance Davis, Cody and Felipe were left.

245

Davis had found meat, coffee, and bread. He started a little fire and made coffee while the others finished loading the bodies. With the others gone, the five men remaining gathered about Davis' fire. They ate hurriedly. The sun was almost down. They knew that it was already out of sight in the valley.

Cody, swallowing his last chunk of bread and meat, spoke to Richards. 'I guess Felipe and I will pull out,' he said.

'Where you goin'?' Richards put down his cup.

'We'll work down through to Paradise,' answered Cody, filling a little sack with coffee. Felipe picked up two tin cups.

'You're in a hell of a hurry,' growled Richards. 'You can't wait, huh?'

Cody shook his head. 'I'd rather not,' he said. 'I got an idea, Richards. It's likely a crazy one but I want to try it.'

Richards nodded. 'You're your own boss,' he answered.

Cody wrapped the coffee in his slicker and tied it to his saddle. Walking John and Felipe's horse had been brought in with the others.

'I'll see you in Bowie,' Cody told Richards. 'Comin', Felipe?'

Felipe had put the tin cups in his saddle roll. He grinned at Richards, nodded to the others and swung up. 'Sure,' he answered Cody's question. 'Con mucho gusto.'

'Take care of yourself, Cody,' warned Wyatt

246

Brown.

Cody mounted Walking John and lifted his hand. 'So long,' he called.

The two rode off, the tired horses shuffling over the rocks. When they were out of sight of the others, Felipe spoke. 'Richards don't like us to go, Cody,' he said.

Cody shook his head. 'No,' he said slowly, 'no, he don't.'

'An' we go? . . .' Felipe was curious.

'Down under Cochise Head,' answered Cody. 'I camped in a cave there one night, Felipe.'

'Si. An'? . . .'

'And I think that's where Clay Stevens will go.'

'We don't get there tonight?'

Again Cody shook his head. 'Not tonight,' he answered with a glance at the darkening sky. 'We'll be up early tomorrow, Felipe.'

Felipe was silent for a moment. Presently he spoke again. 'I got a funny feeling, Cody,' he said. 'I get to thinking about Juan an' about our padre an' la madre. You know, I'm the only one left, Cody.'

Cody looked at his companion. He had known Felipe de Cespedes a long time. As boys they had played together, and, still youngsters, they had gone with the round-up wagons. They were close friends. Each in his own way was successful. Felipe had risen to hold a responsible position with the big THS below the border. Cody was a Deputy United States Marshal.

'Your arm hurt you, Felipe?' asked Cody.

Felipe shook his dark head. 'Es nada,' he said. 'Sometimes I think too much, Cody.'

'An' sometimes I do,' answered Cody.

He felt some premonition, some sense of impending disaster. Felipe's dark face was worried, as if he, too, felt trouble hanging over them.

'Why don't you go back an' go in to town?' questioned Cody suddenly. 'That arm's bad. You ought to have it 'tended to. Why don't you go in, Felipe?'

Felipe's face brightened suddenly. He chuckled a little. 'I was gon' say why don't you go back, Cody,' he announced. 'I feel something bad. I'm bother about it some.'

Cody shrugged. 'I won't go back,' he said slowly. 'An' I reckon you won't. We'll watch each other, compañero. We'll keep a look-out.'

Felipe nodded, his face sobering again. 'Hunch are all right for poor men,' he said. 'Not for you an' me, Cody.' Cody did not reply.

The two companions crossed the ridge and struck down into the dark depths of Pinery Canyon. As they reached the bottom of the slope Cody turned north. They rode a little distance further and Cody stopped Walking John. Felipe drew to a halt beside him.

'Water, food an' grass,' said Cody, voicing the camper's maxim. 'We stop here.'

Felipe dismounted. 'No fire,' he said pointedly.

'An' none in the mornin',' Cody agreed.

Cody unsaddled and hobbled the horses, waving aside Felipe's efforts to help. Felipe's arm bothered him although he hid that fact. The light in the canyon was dim. It was almost dark. In the fading light Cody examined his companion's wound, rebandaging it with a clean cloth from a saddle bag after he had washed the place. The wound was not bleeding, did not appear to be red at its edge. A good clean hole.

The horses contentedly chopped grass along the little creek. Cody stretched out on the sod, let his body relax, rolled and lit a cigarette. Felipe sat, his back against a tree, looking up at the stars that twinkled through the pines' scanty branches.

'Estrellas,' said Felipe. 'Stars, Cody. They bend down close tonight. Mi padre used to say that they were dead men. Maybe Juan is up there.'

Cody made no answer. He had pillowed his head on his arm and his breathing was deep and regular. Cody Venture slept.

The smile that came over Felipe's lips was tender. He straightened his back against the pine tree and felt for his little package of corn husks and his tobacco.

'Bien, amigo,' Felipe said softly. 'I watch for you a while.' A match flamed at the end of the roll of corn husk and smoke trickled from Felipe's nostrils.

Cody did not know how long he slept. He wakened as noiselessly and as effortlessly as he had fallen asleep. There was a spark of light under the black of the pine and Cody rolled over, fully awake, and said, 'Felipe.'

Felipe answered him.

'Why didn't you wake me up?' questioned Cody. 'How long I been asleep?'

'Some time now,' answered de Cespedes. 'It will be morning pretty soon.'

Cody looked at the sky overhead. The stars were already paling.

'Damn it,' said Cody Venture. 'You should have got me up. You been awake all the time?'

'I sleep some,' answered his companion. 'I don't sleep too good anyhow.'

'How's your arm?' asked Cody anxiously.

'Bien. We go on now?'

Cody got up. 'We better,' he said shortly. 'I'll get the horses.'

Felipe rose to his feet. 'We go to Cochise Head,' he said. 'Then we make a fire an' boil coffee. There are two cups in my slicker, Cody.'

Cody did not answer; he had already gone down to the creek after the horses.

Cody looped the ends of the rope he carried about the horses' necks, fastened it, and releasing them from the hobbles, led them back. He saddled Felipe's horse first, and then

Walking John. The gelding swelled under the saddle and Cody dug in a knee and tugged up on the latigo. Felipe ran his hand under his cinch to see if it was tight enough. Cody waited until Felipe had mounted, and then swung up on Walking John. The two rode up the canyon.

There was no talk. The oppression that had hung over them the night before lay like a blanket on them now. Walking John's foot rasped against a rock and the sound echoed loudly.

'You know, Cody,' Felipe's voice was low, 'I think Clay Stevens is the one that killed Juan. I think so.'

'He might of been.' Cody's answer was short. 'He was there, Felipe.'

Felipe said nothing more. They rode in silence for a little distance. Suddenly Cody spoke. 'If we run into him you lay back,' he said sharply. 'I'm an officer, Felipe. Clay is my job.'

Felipe made no answer. Up the canyon the first grey morning lighted Cochise Head. Cody, looking up, wondered if the mass of rocks really resembled the old warrior Cochise: Apache, raider, savage. Treacherous and brave.

Felipe's breath came as a sharp, indrawn hiss. Cody stopped Walking John short. There, under the head, was another light that was not the dawn. It showed red for an instant.

'He's there,' said Felipe quietly.

'We want him alive,' said Cody. 'You wait here, Felipe. I'll try to work past afoot. Give me ten minutes. Then you start up. We'll take him.'

Felipe nodded his understanding and Cody dismounted. Felipe, too, came down from his saddle and Cody tied the horses.

Leaving his companion the young marshal started on north, working noiselessly through the trees that flanked the open bottom of the canyon.

Cody wanted to pass the cave mouth. Then, with Felipe working in from one side and he himself coming from the other, they would take Clay Stevens as he stood by the fire he had so incautiously lighted. A fool, Clay Stevens. A fool to make a fire!

Cody was past the cave mouth now. Carefully, taking what cover he could find, he started up the slope. The ten minutes he had requested were past. Down below Felipe de Cespedes would also be working up the slope. Cody stopped and in the growing light peered out from behind his sheltering tree to see if there was motion on the slope that would disclose Felipe's whereabouts. As he looked a rifle crashed from above and, across the slope of talus that came from the cave, Felipe threw his arms wide and stumbled out.

Clay Stevens was no fool. That fire had been an ambush.

Felipe lay flat on the slope, not moving. Up

above a man laughed tauntingly. Cody was motionless. Again the man laughed and then came Clay Stevens' voice, almost hysterical.

'Got you! Got you, you damn' fool! Thought you could slip in on me.'

The man was to the right of the cave, judging from the direction from which the voice came. Cody stiffened. Clay Stevens called again.

'Come on, Venture. Come on!'

There in that little clump of manzanita! Cody Venture leaped from the shelter of the tree trunk. Caution was forgotten now. Only the desire to kill. To stop that taunting voice forever. Red flame filled Cody's mind but his grey eyes picked out the places for his leaps and his right hand held steady the gun that threw shots at the clump of manzanita.

Clay Stevens was shooting. Bullets tore at Cody's vest. Plucked at the leg of his trousers. One burned hot along his side. He stumbled and went down, his heel caught in a crevice, and as he fell a lead slug whined through the space where his head had been.

Something happened in the manzanita bush. The red branches and the deep green leaves threshed. Clay Stevens came up from behind the manzanita. His rifle was gone but he held a Colt in his hand. Cody struggled up from where he had fallen. He, too, held his Colt. For an instant they faced each other and then Cody's Colt bounced up as its hammer fell. Clay Stevens dropped the gun he held and slowly sank down behind the manzanita. Cody, gun ready, struggled up over the loose talus. He reached the manzanita and looked behind it. Then holstering his gun he ran over the sliding rocks to Felipe de Cespedes.

Felipe's eyes were open. He asked a question as Cody dropped to his knees beside him.

'Stevens?' asked Felipe, his chest heaving as he breathed.

'Dead,' answered Cody. 'I'll get you out of here, Felipe. I'll . . .'

'Amigo mio,' Felipe's words came pantingly. 'Muy bien.'

Cody bent closer. 'All right, boy,' he said. 'All right . . .'

Felipe's lips moved. 'Two cups . . .' he panted. 'In my . . .' The labored breathing ceased and the black eyes closed. Something hot and scalding fell on Cody Venture's hand.

After a time Cody got up. He moved slowly down the slope. He must get the horses, must load the two bodies and try to catch Verne Richards before the sheriff left the rocks. Failing that, there would be the long trip to Bowie. The talus slid under Cody's feet.

CHAPTER EIGHTEEN

Through the Black-Jacks

Tim Auliffe and Arnold Bradford sat on the veranda of the Seven Slash ranchhouse. The sun, striking in from the west, made their faces ruddy but they did not mind the sun. There was a table between the two men and on that table there were papers and two tall glasses.

'I believe that agreement will hold in any court of law,' said Bradford, picking up his glass. 'I practised law in Boston and I'm sure the courts here could not be more stringent than they are in Massachusetts.'

Tim Auliffe looked out over the flat, fenceless expanse of the Sulphur Springs valley, toward the Dragoons, purple in the sunset.

'It'll stand,' he answered. 'Nobody will ever question the pardnership out here.'

Bradford sighed. 'I keep forgetting,' he apologized. 'The West is different from the East. I can't seem to get that into my head.'

'You done pretty well,' announced Auliffe, looking at the other man. 'For a newcomer you done right well. You made a statement in the hospital that you didn't have to make, an' you held a round-up that you didn't have to hold, an' you done several things. I'd consider that you acted mighty neighborly. Particular when I'd made such a damn' fool out of myself.'

Bradford flushed and changed the subject swiftly. 'I had to hold the round-up,' he said. 'The customs men demanded it. I . . .'

'Yeah, I know,' interrupted Auliffe. 'You saved my bacon, too. You an' Cody. If I'd had to tear down my fences with all those D Cross Chihuahuas waitin' to get on the grass, I wouldn't have had a thing. You an' Cody . . .'

'But the customs men have impounded the D Cross cattle for duty payment,' Bradford said precisely. 'They didn't get on the grass long enough to hurt it. I consider it generous of you, Auliffe, to take me into partnership. You and Cody Venture . . .'

'We'll be kissin' each other next,' grunted Tim Auliffe. 'I promised Timmy I wouldn't drink again, but I reckon this calls for a little celebration.' He rose from his chair and bellowed. 'Bill! Oh, Bill!'

From somewhere in the rear Bill Longee answered.

'Bring that demijohn here,' roared Tim Auliffe. 'An' don't stop an' drink it dry before you get here!'

Bill Longee's reply was unintelligible.

'I feel as though I were to blame for the whole thing,' Bradford spoke softly. 'I didn't know men. I hired Clay Stevens and in doing that I caused a great deal of trouble and the death of some good men. I . . .'

Bill Longee came around the corner of the veranda carrying a jug. He set it down and stood surlily surveying his employer.

'There's goin' to be a dance Saturday,' announced Bill Longee. 'At Lance Blount's. He wants me an' Bar Fly to play for it.'

'Go ahead an' play.' Tim Auliffe was carefully pouring from the demijohn into Bradford's glass. 'Go ahead. That's all you're good for. Mebbe we'll all go over.'

Bill Longee snorted and retired from the porch. He had expected an argument, at least a warning not to get drunk.

'Here's how,' said Tim Auliffe, raising his glass.

The men drank. Bradford put his glass back on the table. 'Now,' he resumed, 'with our holdings together we ought to have a fine ranch. I was particularly pleased when you agreed to take Cody into partnership with us. I...'

'If you hadn't suggested it, I would have,' grunted Big Tim. 'We need Cody to run things. Now that he's quit that marshal job he'll mebbe amount to somethin'.'

Bradford smiled quietly and Tim Auliffe caught the look.

'As a cowman,' he amended hastily.

'They ought to be here,' said Bradford, shading his eyes against the sun with an upraised hand. 'Timmy said they wouldn't go far.'

'Cody told me that he wanted to go to your place,' replied Tim. 'Still they ought to be in pretty soon.' He too, shaded his eyes with his hand and peered beneath it.

Boot heels clumped and Johnny Bowen came around the corner of the porch. 'Them broncs, Mister Auliffe,' said Johnny Bowen, 'you want I should turn 'em to the horse pasture or . . .'

'Ask Cody,' snapped Tim Auliffe.

Johnny Bowen lifted his eyebrows, grinned as he saw the glasses, and retired the way he had come.

'Ought to be gettin' here,' said Tim again. 'It ain't a day's ride to the Circle B. They ought . . . Here they are.'

Two horses appeared at the bend of the canyon. They were close together, a big dark bay gelding, and a bright sorrel. The riders were as near each other as the horses would permit. As the two men on the porch stared, a girl's laugh came, high and clear and carefree. A man's deeper mirth echoed it.

Cody Venture and his bride were coming home, through the black-jacks.

Chivers Large Print Direct

If you have enjoyed this Large Print book and would like to build up your own collection of Large Print books and have them delivered direct to your door, please contact **Chivers Large Print Direct**.

Chivers Large Print Direct offers you a full service:

✧ **Created to support your local library**

✧ **Delivery direct to your door**

✧ **Easy-to-read type and attractively bound**

✧ **The very best authors**

✧ **Special low prices**

For further details either call Customer Services on 01225 443400 or write to us at

Chivers Large Print Direct
FREEPOST (BA 1686/1)
Bath
BA1 3QZ